GHOST

Steel Patriots MC

Book One

Mary Kennedy

III
INSATIABLE INK

Editing provided by: pccProofreading

Contents

CHAPTER ONE

Eric "Ghost" Stanton kicked the gravel once more as if by doing so, he would discover a clue into what fucking went wrong with this op. He ran his long, tattooed fingers through his dark hair and let a slew of expletives fly that had the heads of all his men turning to stare at him. He didn't acknowledge the stares, nor did they expect him to.

The twelve kidnapped girls were supposed to be in this house, yet when they'd arrived, he and his team found nothing except one lost shoe and a handful of broken crayons. The intel had been good but apparently not good enough. The girls, all under the age of nine, were kidnapped from their school and had been moved from one location to the next, with the kidnappers demanding an unreasonable ransom from their poor parents.

"Ghost?" He heard his name but couldn't seem to answer. "Ghost? What the fuck do we do now? We can't stay here."

Tyler "Tango" Green was his second-in-command and most trusted friend. They'd survived BUDs together, becoming Navy SEALs, where for the last fifteen years, they'd done their best to stop the spread of evil in this world.

His whole team were men he trusted with his own life. They were the best trained and the most respected. A unit of mixed Special Forces sent into the worst possible parts of the world to undo the most fucked up crimes. Except lately, it felt as though they were banging their heads against the wall.

"Ghost!?" yelled Tango once more.

"What the fuck? What?" he yelled back at his friend.

Tango stood tight-lipped wanting to let the curses and smart retorts fly, but he just couldn't, not after what Whiskey just found. Wade "Whiskey" English, a Marine Sniper and one badass fighter was tough as shit, which is why Tango was trying to control his smartass mouth in this moment. If Whiskey was upset, something was wrong.

"Whiskey found something. He says we need to get there now, five hundred yards east around the bend."

Ghost nodded, following his second-in-command, his steps brisk and sure. He rolled the information around in his head. Their contact at base told them the girls were moved from their small school where they'd been kept as hostages for the last week to this extraction point.

Ghost and his team were to kill the kidnappers and bring the girls home to their village. From the start, everything seemed wrong. The information was too easy, too straightforward. Typically, kidnappers of girls in these countries didn't want ransoms. They knew the families couldn't afford it. They usually wanted to sell the girls.

But it was more than that. There were no roadblocks or watchers along the way, and when they arrived at the location, it was obvious why. The girls were moved again.

Ghost followed Tango, kicking the gravel once more as they made the bend in the road. He stopped because Whiskey was stopped in front of him. Following his friends' gaze upward, he saw why the entire team was planted in the middle of the road. Twelve little girls, twelve innocent little girls, were hanging from the cliff-side, naked, beaten, cut, and God knew what else.

Their tiny bodies were bloated, flies and buzzards feeding from their open wounds. Ghost pulled his side-arm and fired into the air, not caring who heard, only hoping to chase away the carcass-eating birds. Innocence. Innocence lost.

"Cut them down," he said, looking at his team. "Cut them down, and we'll bury them. Their parents don't need to see this."

"Then what?" asked Doc.

Jack "Doc" Harris was the finest field medic anyone had ever seen, but also an Army Ranger. He'd single-handedly saved every man on board a crashed helicopter by improvising, using spare parts on board the chopper when his own medical supplies began to dwindle. When the team was formed, Ghost knew he had to have him.

"Then we hunt these motherfuckers down and kill every last one of them."

Ghost knew it would end their careers. He looked up at all his men, Whiskey, Doc, Tango, Gunner, Zulu, and Razor. Six of the finest fighting machines on the planet. He waited for one of them to turn and go in the opposite direction. There would be no judgment for this. Their mission was technically over. The girls were to be brought back alive, and if found dead, the team was to return to base. By going after the kidnappers, they would be violating their orders, and they all knew what that would mean.

"Let's kill some people," said Gunner casually.

After cutting the girls down, Ghost made the decision to return them, as is, to their families. They would want something to grieve over, not just memories. No matter how painful it might be, if one of the girls were his child, he would want to bury her. The girls were carefully laid out in the back of the truck, and tarps covered their small bodies. Ghost instructed the driver to return to base slowly, so as to give the team the time they needed.

The young soldier who volunteered as transport knew what the team was going to do and knew that he would do the same thing if the circumstances were reversed. With a kid sister at home who was the same age as these girls, he knew he would have lost his shit.

It took them three days of trudging through desert brush, mountain trails, and finally crossing a tiny river to find the kidnappers in a small house. The vermin never dreamed the Americans would follow them, so they were ill-prepared for the onslaught coming their way.

Four men were disposed of quickly on the outside of the house as Ghost's team worked efficiently, doing what they do best, ridding the world of sick bastards. On the inside, two more were raping a young woman, her body already depleted of life.

Ghost snapped the neck of the first man before the second could even grab his pants. Whiskey held the man by his upper arms, pulling back sharply, hearing the snap of bones in his shoulders. He screamed in pain, begging for mercy.

"Mercy? You want fucking mercy, you piece of shit?" asked Tango. "Did you give those little girls mercy? Did you stop when they cried for their parents? No. You didn't. And neither will I." Tango took his time, breaking as many bones as he could before finally using his knife to carve the man into pieces. Ghost gave the order to blow the house before they left, ensuring that the evidence of the men was gone. But it didn't matter.

Two months later, they were 'asked' to leave the service of their country before formal charges were brought against them for disobeying a direct order. Ghost was thirty-nine years old. He'd served his country in good faith for almost half his life. Now, he was headed home.

"Where will you go, Ghost?" asked Whiskey.

Ghost looked at the men he'd called teammates for the last decade. Each man was hand-selected for his team, partly because he knew of their skills, but mostly because he trusted them with his life and the lives of every member of the team.

"I have a proposition for all of you. I know some of you have family back home, but nobody has an old lady that I'm aware of," he said, smirking at the men on the transport.

"Well, Tango has a mule he's fond of," said Doc with a smile.

"Fuck you, Doc, at least it's a female mule," he grinned. "So, what's your point, Ghost?"

"My point is, when my Pops died, he left me a huge piece of land. It's nothing special, but it's got an old garage on the property where he used to repair cars, bikes, tractors, shit like that for neighbors. The house burned down years ago, but Pops made the barn into a pretty livable space."

"Sooooo, you want us all to live there?" asked Gunner.

"No. I mean, yea. Look, I ride, you all know that, and I know that most of you do too. What if... what if we formed our own club... motorcycle club? We pick a name, make the garage something that we can all work and maybe open a bar or some shit."

The men all looked at one another nodding. It was a good idea, but not one of them knew anything about running a business or a bar.

"I'm in," said Tango, "but I know jack-shit about operating a bar. I can fix anything with a motor and so can most of you but a bar? I don't know, man. I know *how* to drink, just not how to mix drinks."

"Look, it doesn't have to happen right away. MCs are pretty territorial. We need to make sure we're not stepping on anyone's toes. I'm not a fan of becoming an outlaw MC. We got our taste of outlaw in that fucking shithole we just came from, and it didn't do any of us any good. I'm suggesting that between the bar and the garage, we'll have two legitimate businesses. Maybe on the side we sort of informally help people."

"Help people? Like good Samaritans?" asked Gunner.

"Sort of. I'm thinking more like we take jobs others won't, but only the ones we want to take. We find lost kids, kidnap victims. We help the old lady being screwed over by a nasty landlord. Shit like that." The men all looked at him, raising their eyebrows.

"Look, I know we've spent our entire careers doing just this kind of shit, but now we get to do it on our terms. The shop needs cleaning up, and the barn will need to be made habitable, adding more electrical, plumbing, that sort of shit, but it's huge. I've got a shit-ton of money saved from all my deployments, and Pops left me a nice little chunk of change."

"And we'd be partners?" asked Whiskey.

"Yea, we'd be fucking partners. We'd be brothers, asshole," he said with a grin. "Just like we are now. We'd rely on one another and do shit our way. No red tape, no governments telling us what to do. We ride our fucking bikes when we want. We take the jobs we want. We fuck who we want, and we drink 'til we can't drink no more." The men smiled in his direction.

"I'm in," said Tango.

"Me too," said Doc.

"Why the fuck not?" said Razor.

"Fuck, you know I'm in, asshole," said Gunner.

"I guess we need a name," said Whiskey. "How about Steel Soldiers?"

"No fucking way, asshole. I'm a SEAL, not a fucking soldier," said Tango.

The others laughed and nodded. They were all from different branches of the military and loved teasing each other about the superiority of their own branch but deep down held mad respect for one another.

"Steel Patriots," said Ghost. "The steel between our legs and the fucking patriot spirit we all still carry."

"Steel Patriots…" whispered Whiskey. The others nodded and smiled.

"Steel Patriots it is."

CHAPTER TWO

Seven Years Later...

"So, the women have all been returned to their families. Hell, most of them weren't women yet. They were just fucking teenagers." Gunner gripped the arm of the chair, and a cracking sound was heard in the room. Doc settled a hand on his forearm to calm the man.

"I know it's hard, brother, but we have to remember that these girls all did something utterly stupid as well. I mean, some guy invites you to a party with free booze and food, and you jump on it not even knowing the asshole? It's fucked up. I'm not saying the girls deserved it, but maybe we need to think about doing some education on this shit?" Doc shook his head remembering the physical state of some of the young girls.

"I know what you're saying, Doc," said Ghost, "but we can't be all things to all people. I mean, we're doing a stellar fucking business in the garage, the bar is making money, and the jobs we take on the side are affording us the chance to build houses on the property. I don't think we can take on anymore right now."

"I agree," said Tango, "besides, we have another issue, well, situation that could become an issue. The Warriors have asked to meet with us."

"Why would that be an issue?" asked Gunner. "We've done work with them before, and it's always turned out pretty well."

"It has, but this time they want to discuss what happened with those young women. It seems they had a piece of that pie, and they weren't happy about us stopping it."

"Are you fucking kidding me?" said Ghost, standing at the head of the table. His fist slammed down hard enough to cause the table to shake. "Are you fucking telling me they're dealing in flesh now?"

"That's what I said, but they claim they only allowed for clear passage through their territory. They didn't *technically* deal in the flesh. I say toma-toe, tomato, but they're pissed and want to chat."

"Jesus Christ, when?" asked Ghost.

"They haven't said yet. I get the feeling they're dealing with some internal issues of their own. You know how those guys are. It's a bunch of one tour soldier wannabees, and they think they're fucking king of the pyramid. My contact there said he'd let me know when their prez wants to meet."

"Fine. Fucking fine, whatever. Did we get a replacement for the late shift at the bar yet?" asked Ghost.

"No," said Razor, shaking his head. "I have the younger guys covering shifts now. The twins, Eagle and Hawk, are doing most of the shifts. They're not bad, but it's not what they want to do going forward."

"I don't give a fuck if it's what they want to do going forward. They're the fucking new guys and will do what we say until we tell them not to!" He slammed the table again and took a deep breath. Seven years it took them to get to this point where they were making money legitimately, enjoying life and living the way they'd always wanted to... on their terms. Ghost was forty-six years old now. Forty-fucking-six and most days felt it.

He worked hard with his brothers, got as much pussy as he could handle because no matter how old he was, his dick was still huge, and chicks loved it. He didn't spend the night, and he didn't kiss, ever. Suck my dick or fuck me, always protected. But that was it. He got his rocks off and kicked them out. He didn't need the distraction or the drama.

"Alright, everyone, quiet night tonight with just the MC in the bar. George is cooking ribs tonight, and we're just gonna fucking chill for the night. We deserve it. See everyone back here at seven."

Nods of approval were heard around the table, and everyone turned to leave, except Tango. He waited until the last man was out the door and turned toward his friend.

"You okay, Ghost?" he asked. Ghost lifted his head and stared at his friend for a few minutes, saying nothing.

"Yea, fuck yea, I'm good, brother. Getting fucking old and this shit with the Warriors doesn't sit well with me. They're fucking dirty, and I want no part of their shit." He took a deep breath and rubbed his chest as if there were an ache deep inside. "I don't know, man; I just feel like there's something coming, and I can't put my finger on it."

"Well, we both know that if we listen to that voice, it pays off."

Ghost nodded as his friend left the meeting room. He walked into the hallway, staring toward the back of the barn. When they'd decided this is where they would live and work, they'd expanded the building to four times its original size. Along the back, facing the vast forested property, was a long porch with chairs and rockers to enjoy the cool breezes of the evening. Most of the men liked staying in good physical condition, so trails were carved weaving through the trees, around trickling streams, and back toward the barn.

Ghost stepped outside, seeing George at the massive pit covered in ribs. He nodded at the older man and took in a lungful of clean mountain air. He loved this part of Virginia. They were always cool enough without being cold all the time. They had decent summer temps, beautiful fall colors, and snow in the winter, but not too much. They were only a few hours to the beach and the big cities, but their little piece of heaven was perfect as far as he was concerned.

He rubbed his chest once more and took another deep breath. Heading back inside, he made his way to his apartment upstairs and decided to rest before the party. Rest. That's what he needed, just a little rest.

CHAPTER THREE

Grace Easton smiled at the faces of her twin daughters laughing with one another. Their contagious excitement filtered her way. Their friends were expected later for the party, but her parents should arrive any time now.

Hope and Faith were celebrating their high school graduation today, and Grace could not have been prouder. The girls were fraternal twins but still looked incredibly alike. Their long honey-colored hair and sparkling green eyes laughed with every word they shared.

"Grandma and Grandpa are here!" yelled Faith. She ran to the front door to let the older couple in and was smothered in loving hugs.

"Oh, let me look at my girls," said Henry. "Look at 'em, Val. Look at 'em!"

"I would if you'd get outta my way," she said, shoving his arm. "You two look beautiful, just beautiful! Are you ready for your trip?"

"We are soooo ready, Grandma," said Hope. "We leave the day after tomorrow. Mom even upgraded us to first-class tickets! Can you believe it? We'll be gone for a whole month backpacking around Europe. We're going to London first…"

Grace heard her daughter's voice drift off as she led her grandparents out to the patio decorated with Chinese lanterns, streamers, and signs congratulating all the graduates. She smiled at the girls as they excitedly told the story of the upcoming adventure. Looking at the clock, Grace cursed.

"Damn! Mom! Dad!" she yelled through the screen door. "I have to go pick up the cake. I'll be back in about an hour, okay?"

"Go ahead, honey," said Henry. "We've got this."

"Love you guys!" she yelled back.

Grace smiled at her father, holding hands with Hope while her mother held hands with Faith. They were as close as any grandparents and grandchildren could be. She dropped the apron on the counter and headed toward the garage where her old SUV was waiting. Now that the girls were off to college, maybe she could look into trading it in for something newer.

As the manager of a local restaurant, she made a decent living, but in the last ten years, she'd put every penny she had into a college fund for the girls. It hadn't been easy, but she made do with last year's winter coat and boots more years than she could count. She'd skipped out on girls' nights, had a friend trim her hair for her, and didn't indulge in anything that wasn't necessary.

Grace bit her lip, remembering the day her ex-husband forced her hand, making her demand that he leave the house and their family. The girls were just eight years old then, eight and wondering when their daddy might come home again. They stopped wondering after the third time he'd shown up drunk trying to hit their mother. Grace filed a restraining order and received full custody of the girls after that.

Kyle went away quietly for the most part. Every year or so, he would rear his ugly head and cause a scene, but for the most part, he'd behaved. Which is why the number popping up on her screen sent shivers down her spine. Don't answer it. Don't answer it. Shit!

"Hello."

"I want to see the girls," he said.

"Nice to speak to you too, Kyle, and no."

"Fuck you, Grace! I want to see my girls today of all days. I know they graduated, and you didn't even fucking invite me!"

"I did invite you to the ceremony, Kyle, but your invite was mailed back to me. Apparently, you moved but never told me, so don't blame me. The girls deserve to have their day, Kyle, and they asked that I not track you down to invite you. I'm sorry, but you brought this on yourself." Grace tried to remain calm. She didn't want to lose it and then have the girls know that something was wrong.

"You fucking whore! You fucking bitch of a whore!" He was screaming so loudly Grace pulled the phone away from her ear. She placed the SUV in park and waited until his tirade was finished before going into the bakery. "Remember, Grace, you did this, you did this!"

The line went dead, and chills ran up Grace's arms. Jesus, will this ever get easier. Stepping inside the bakery, the young girl behind the counter asked for her name and told her it would be just another few minutes on the cake as they were putting the final touches on the design. Grace smiled and nodded at the young girl, taking a seat.

Kyle. What a bastard. They'd met in college while Grace was studying business. Kyle wasn't in school, but he was working at the dealership where she bought her first car. He'd asked her to dinner, and she accepted. By the time she'd graduated, he was proposing.

Grace turned him down the first two times, but when she discovered she was pregnant, she felt it was the right thing to do. It wasn't until later that Kyle admitted to tampering with her birth control pills.

Grace was furious and yet couldn't be angry for the beautiful gifts of Faith and Hope. As the years went on, Kyle moved from one job to the next, always making excuses for why he'd been fired this time. Drunk on the job, caught with marijuana in the bathroom, or the best and final one, fucking the receptionist in the supply closet. That's when Grace knew it was done. She'd filed for divorce and sole custody, moved in with her parents until she could afford a place of their own and devoted herself fully to the girls.

Something in Kyle's voice had Grace feeling unsettled. Paying for the cake, she set it in the back of the SUV and picked up her phone calling her mom. No answer. She tried Faith and then Hope, still no answer. Shit! She picked up speed, making her way through their little town toward her house. Three blocks away, she saw the lights and knew, she just knew.

Grace slammed on the brakes in front of her house and took off running toward the front door. An officer was standing guard and grabbed her around the waist.

"Ma'am, ma'am, you can't go in there…"

"It's my house! My daughters… where are my daughters…" she yelled.

A female officer turned toward the noise and nodded at the man who was holding her. Grace raced toward the back patio and stopped. Blood covered the back deck, thick puddles of crimson-colored liquid oozing from beneath the bodies, dripping between the weathered boards. White sheets covered five bodies… five…

She saw her mother's delicate hand peeking from beneath one of the sheets, her wedding ring of nearly fifty years still on her well-manicured finger. Then her father's shoes. The sensible, ugly, awful black shoes they always teased him about.

"No… no…" she whispered, clutching herself around the waist. The pain in her chest turning to fire.

"Ms. Easton… Ms. Easton," said the woman standing beside her. "Ms. Easton, I'm so very sorry… so very, very sorry."

The hands of her daughters were locked together, hands clasped as they were entering this world, the same way as they were exiting this world.

"Wh-what…"

"Your neighbor, Mr. Yang," she said, pointing to the fifth sheet, "he heard gunshots and called 911, but then ran over to see if he could help. Witnesses said your ex-husband, Kyle Easton, was seen leaving the scene with several weapons."

"K-Kyle? He c-called me… he wanted to… he wanted to come to the party. The girls… oh God," she stuttered, tears falling freely down her face now. "The girls didn't want him here, so I told him no. He said I would regret it. He said it was my fault."

"What was your fault?" asked the female officer.

"This," she said, spreading her arms, "he said this would be my fault. That's what he meant." Her knees hit the deck, and she sobbed uncontrollably. "No! Noooooo!" she yelled.

Grace crawled toward the clasped hands of her daughters, sticky red liquid clinging to her fingers; she placed their hands between her own. She curled her body between the two lifeless bodies of her children… the children she bore… the children she raised and loved and cherished. She held to the cold hands and wept, screaming at the sky and God, anyone who would listen, anyone who would bring her daughters back to her.

CHAPTER FOUR

Grace stood over the four graves, the caskets all now completely lowered into the cold dirt. Flowers covered the sites, huge sprays of roses, lilies, and daisies. Daisies were the girls' favorite flower. The Priest held her hand, saying something that Grace couldn't even understand. She only nodded, begging to be free to go home, home where she'd yet to be able to wipe the blood from the deck or to open her daughters' rooms and unpack their bags. Home where she no longer felt safe or protected. Home.

She never even noticed the cars as they pulled away. Detective Sanders moved closer to her and lightly touched her elbow, jarring her from her thoughts.

"Ms. Easton, again, we're so very sorry for your losses. I know this is an unbelievably difficult time for you..."

"Did you find him?" she asked, stopping the detective mid-sentence. "Did you find my ex-husband? Did you find Kyle?"

"Ma'am, we're looking everywhere. The entire state of Alabama, as well as the country now has a photo of the man, and they're looking for him." She nodded and turned to move toward her vehicle. "Ms. Easton? Grace!" She stopped and turned to look at the man.

"Grace, we think he might come for you next. Let us put a few patrol cars outside your house."

"No, let him come."

Grace heard him calling her again, but she refused to turn around. Making her way back to her home, she entered the dark house and closed all the blinds, locking the doors and windows. She'd refused to have a wake. Refused to have people parading through and spewing their "I'm sorry" when there was nothing anyone could do to bring back her girls and her parents.

She picked up the bottle of Jameson and headed toward her bedroom. No one could make it right again, no one. Her last thought was an absurd one that she wasn't even sure why she was having. Run. It's all she kept thinking, all she kept feeling, run.

"Wake up! Wake up!" yelled the voice in her ear.

Grace stirred slightly, crying out as she did. Her body was on fire from the top of her head to the tips of her toes. The first thing she noticed was that her black dress she wore to the funeral was in a pile in the corner of the tiny room. Looking down at her own body, she saw that indeed she was only wearing a bra, her panties in shreds on the floor.

She also noticed the slashes on her torso, across her abdomen and legs, the bruises up and down her chest and legs.

"There you are, you fucking cunt! I told you it would be your fault. I told you," he smiled at her, a lecherous, disgusting smile. Dear God. He'd killed his own children... he was keeping her...

"You killed my daughters, my children, your daughters!" she yelled. Grace tried to move but realized she was cuffed to a small pipe that ran up the side of the wall. "You disgust me!"

"I disgust you? You traitorous whore! You left me! I make one mistake fucking that girl, and you left me! Who does that?"

"It wasn't one mistake, Kyle, and you know it," she said quietly. She noticed the glint of the knife at his side, barely concealed in his pants pocket and swallowed hard. "You made lots of mistakes, too many to even remember."

"I will kill you." His face was enflamed, the red spreading to his ears and covering his neck and chest.

"Fine," she said calmly, "kill me. I have nothing anymore. The girls were my life... my parents... you took it all from me, all of it."

He screamed a feral, animal-like scream slamming his fist against the side of her head. She tried to block the blow, but it was too much, snapping her head back. Now he had a clear line to her jaw, then down her body yelling as he did.

Grace reached for the knife hanging from his pocket. Pulling it free, she brought it down hard on the top of his shoulder. It wasn't lethal, but it was enough to stop him while she kicked his face with all the strength she possessed. It was hard enough that he passed out.

"Oh God! Oh God, what now, what now?" she cried. *Think, Grace... think.*

Grace reached as far as she could, afraid if she touched him, he would wake. She kicked him with her toes once, twice, and then again, and he only moaned. Scrambling as close as she could, she pulled his body closer, searching his pockets for the key to the handcuffs. She found the key in his shirt pocket along with her SUV keys. That's how he'd gotten her here.

Grace uncuffed herself and then cuffed him to the pipe. Feeling for his wallet, she found it in his back pocket and pulled out the cash he had, three hundred and twelve dollars. She grabbed her black dress and stood, painfully taking in gulps of air. Her torso was littered with bruises, and she knew her ribs were most likely broken. Her face hurt, her legs on fire from the cuts he'd sliced into her skin. She looked around the room for anything she might use as a weapon, finding nothing. She opened the door slowly.

It was pitch black outside giving her no indication of where they might be. She had no idea what day it was or what time, but she knew she needed to get as far away from here as she possibly could.

She slipped the dress over her head and realized that Kyle had ripped the zipper, so it would only cover her front. In the seat of her SUV, she finally felt somewhat safe.

Grace had no clue where she was going or where she was currently located, she just drove, endless miles of roads and trees, no houses, no police, just backroads… in a deep fog of hazy visions and horrific memories. The faded road signs she'd never seen before flew by her vision, each mile bringing more pain, her vision blurring from hunger and the agony wracking her body. Two days of non-stop driving except to get gas, and Grace felt it coming, the darkness that would envelop her for good. Her life was slipping away.

She felt the impact of the SUV against the tree, her head now bleeding from a new wound. *Great!* That's all she needed was one more wound. Stepping from the vehicle, she began walking in her bare feet.

I can't stop… he'll find me… I can't stop…

Grace wasn't sure how long it was before she spotted the lights of a large building ahead. There was a garage out front and a fence running behind it, where a large barn-like structure stood. She smelled the food and her stomach growled. Seeing the gate, she walked slowly toward it and a young man standing at the opening.

"Hey, lady, this is private… Oh fuck!" He picked up the radio and mumbled something into it.

"H-help…"

CHAPTER FIVE

"So, Gunner decides that this chick might be THE one for him. I mean, it's fucking bike week at Daytona. There's not a fucking woman there that's looking for anything permanent, and he thinks he's found the one," said Ghost, laughing at his friend.

"Fuck you, asshole. She was serious about me," he smiled.

"Yea, her and her three friends who wanted to fuck you and rob you in that room," said Doc. "Good thing I came in with condoms, or they would have had you for sure."

"Wait, you walked in with condoms?" asked Hawk.

"Yea, the asshole texted me on the way up to their room that he needed a whole box, so being the good teammate and brother that I am, I ran them up to him. Just in time to catch the four little sluts tying his ass to the bed and fingering through his wallet. He was fucking knocked out thanks to the drinks they mixed for him."

"Lesson learned," said Gunner, shrugging his shoulders. The squelch of the two-way radio sounded next to him, and he picked it up. "This better be fucking good, newbie!"

"I have a woman at the front... I... I need Doc... oh God... get Doc!" his voice wavered, and his twin leapt from the chair running toward the front, but not before Ghost, Gunner, and Tango. They raced around the barn headed to the front gate but could see Eagle with a woman in his arms. Ghost swallowed, his stomach threatening to empty its contents.

"She... she walked toward the gate and only said 'help' before she passed out," he said, handing the woman to Ghost. He looked down at her beaten face and cringed. She was covered in blood, old and new. The black dress was dirty and torn, but it didn't go without notice that it was also ripped, most likely by a knife.

"Get her inside for Doc," said Gunner.

Ghost carried the woman toward the barn, through the bar toward the backrooms reserved for the team. Making his way upstairs, he lay her in the guest room at the end of the hall. Doc stormed through, turning on the overhead light.

"Holy fucking hell," he whispered. "Out of my way! Tango? Get me some water and clean cloths. Gunner? Get my big kit. The one I brought isn't going to cut it."

"Jesus, Doc, I've never seen anyone…" whispered Ghost.

Doc only nodded, immediately going to work on the woman. Ghost and the team stood nearby racing from the room when Doc needed something, returning with it quickly. He cleaned each wound, dressing it or stitching it as needed. He rolled the woman to her side, and they all heard the moans of pain from that simple movement.

"I need to check and see if she's been raped," he said, turning toward the men.

They all turned their bodies to face the wall, effectively saying they refused to leave but would not watch while Doc examined the woman. It felt as though it took hours, but a few moments later, he cleared his throat and the men all turned back.

"It doesn't appear she was raped, but there is bruising on the inside of her thighs. My guess is she's between thirty-five and forty, but honestly, I can't tell with all the damage done to her face. Her nose was broken, but I've set that. She has multiple cuts and contusions, a pretty nasty head wound which is recent, so maybe she got in an accident nearby."

"I'll send someone to check the roads," said Tango. Ghost nodded at his friend, his eyes never leaving the battered body of the woman.

"She has some nasty chafing on one wrist which indicates to me she was being held against her will somewhere. She's malnourished and dehydrated, but the IV should help with that."

"Can we get prints?" asked Ghost.

"Not right now," said Doc. "Her hands have been pretty abused. It's like someone intentionally stepped on her hands, or they're defensive wounds. A few of the finger pads have been burned as well. Her face is so messed up, I'm afraid to try and do dental impressions."

Ghost nodded his head again, staring at the woman. Her dark brown hair touched just below her shoulders, the dirt and blood caked in the strands.

"Ghost?" He looked up at Doc, not realizing he'd been calling his name. "I'm going to see if I can get a hold of one of the hang-arounds to come and help me clean her up."

"No, no, I'll help you do that."

Doc opened his mouth to protest, but Ghost growled low in his chest at his friend, not even recognizing what he'd done. Doc nodded and moved toward the bathroom filling the sink with warm water. Ghost watched him and then turned seeing the poor woman's filthy body.

"Let's stand her in the shower," said Ghost, removing his shirt. He removed his boots next and then his jeans, pulling off his boxers. His ripped arms and chest flexed as he moved toward the woman. Doc could only nod, turning on the warm water.

"You hold her, and I'll wash her hair and body. Poor thing won't want to wake up like this."

Ghost only nodded, staring down at the woman's face. He had no idea what she really looked like, no clue what color her eyes were, or whether or not she had straight or crooked teeth. But for whatever reason, it didn't matter. Nothing mattered in that moment except the warm body in his arms.

Ghost felt Doc wiping her body, gently trying to remove the crusted blood and dirt, and then he moved to her hair. Ghost turned slightly, letting her hair fall under the spray. Doc gently washed her hair and then conditioned it, rinsing as best he could. Grabbing a towel, he squeezed the water from her hair and then carefully rubbed her wet body dry.

Ghost lay her down on the bed, and Doc covered her naked form.

"Go change, Ghost," said Doc quietly. "She'll be out for a while. I've given her something for pain. I'm not leaving."

Ghost nodded and headed down the hall, naked, his clothes in his hands. He moved toward his room and opened the dresser, pulling out his favorite khaki shorts and a t-shirt. Slipping on a pair of running shoes, he moved back down the hall to the room.

Coming up the stairs were Tango, Eagle, and Hawk.

"We drove ten miles both ways and saw nothing. I can't believe she could have walked any further than that, but we can go look again tomorrow." Ghost nodded.

"Get some sleep, it's late. Doc and I will sit with her," he said calmly. Tango looked at his friend, worry etched in his features.

"She'll be okay, Ghost. Doc will make sure of it."

"Who could do that to her, Tango? Who the fuck would do that to a woman?" he asked his friend.

"I don't know, brother, but we'll figure it out."

Ghost opened the door to see Doc sitting in the big chair in the corner. He had blood all over his shirt and looked utterly exhausted. Looking at the clock, Ghost realized that they'd been working on the woman for nearly four hours.

"I'll sit with her, Doc. Go get a shower. I'll find you if anything changes." He nodded, leaving the room, quietly closing the door behind him. Ghost watched the woman for a minute, her shallow breathing causing the sheet to rise and fall, her small breasts barely moving. She moaned an incomprehensible sound, and Ghost pulled the chair closer to the bed.

"It's okay, sweetheart. It's okay. You're safe. I promise you, you're safe." He held her tiny hand in his and rubbed his big, callused thumb along the back of her skin. "Who hurt you like this? Who did this to you?"

No worries, baby. I will find him and when I do, he'll wish he'd taken the fast track to hell.

CHAPTER SIX

Pain was everywhere. It was filling her body from every possible point of contact. Her head felt as though it might roll off of her shoulders, her shoulders feeling as though they weren't even attached to her body. Her legs were on fire, her abdomen and chest painful to even take a breath. She tried to move her mouth, open it to call for help, and immediately regretted making that decision. The stabs of agony filled her body, and she moaned.

The memory... the memory came back. Kyle. He'd taken her, beat her, tried to rape her, but he couldn't get it up; typical Kyle, she thought even through her pain. He'd chained her to the wall, hit her, cut her and... killed her family. He'd killed everyone.

She felt the coolness of the sheet over her body and wondered if Kyle had a change of heart. Then she remembered stabbing him, leaving him cuffed to the pipe. She remembered driving, driving nowhere... anywhere and the car crashing... she walked and walked. Oh God! Where am I?

"Shhhhh, it's okay, baby girl. It's okay," said the deep baritone voice. It washed over her like smooth bourbon, silky and smoky. "You're safe. It's all okay now."

"N-not safe... never..." she tried to talk, but it was so painful, she couldn't continue, tears rolling down her cheeks.

"Don't try to talk, baby girl. It's okay. You're safe here."

She turned her head with great effort and tremendous pain toward the sound of her savior. He was tall; even seated, she could tell he was tall, and he was well-muscled. He had tattoos up and down both arms and on his hands. His hair was slightly longer on top, shaved closer on the sides, his full beard framing a deliciously sexy mouth.

"My name is Ghost, Eric, but my teammates and brothers call me Ghost. You don't have to tell me your name yet if you don't want to. We're just going to get you well and keep you safe, okay?" She blinked her eyes twice, more tears falling from the beautiful green depths. Green. They were green, he thought.

"Don't cry, sugar. You're breaking my heart here," he said, smiling at her. He heard a throat clearing from behind him and turned to see his friends Doc and Tango standing in the door, grinning. "Look, you have company, sugar. This is Doc. He put you back together. And that's Tango. He's part of this team, and he's going to make sure you're safe, too."

"That's right, honey, no worries while you're here. Me or one of the boys will always be here to protect you." He tried to smile at the woman on the bed, but it was crushing his soul to see her beaten, broken body.

"How are you feeling?" asked Doc, sitting beside her on the bed. She blinked once, indicating not okay, and he nodded. "I know, honey. You have some pretty serious injuries, but we're going to get you there. Can you tell us your name?"

"Gr... Grace," she whispered through a jaw that was barely able to open.

"Grace," said Ghost, smiling down at her. "Well, that seems a fitting name. Grace. Beautiful name for a beautiful lady." The man Tango nodded at her and turned, leaving the room.

Grace looked up at the big man and wanted to scream. She wanted to tell him to help her kill Kyle. Find Kyle and kill him. But she couldn't; she couldn't move her mouth; she couldn't move her mind; she couldn't even make her heart feel the pain she'd felt only days before... or was it weeks before now? All sense of time was lost.

She knew from the big man she'd been asleep now for four days, which meant she'd been gone from her home for more than two weeks. She remembered hearing the date on the radio while she drove and was shocked to know that Kyle had kept her for almost ten days. Her body believed it. It felt like ten days of beatings and abuse, but her mind was struggling to wrap her head around that.

In all that time, was there no one who reported her missing? What about the restaurant? Great indication that you need a damn life!

Now knowing that she'd been here four days, she couldn't even feel the pain still filling her chest. Her daughters, her beautiful, talented daughters were gone. Her parents, her loving, amazing parents were no longer here to help her. Gone. Everything and everyone were gone.

Bits and pieces of Kyle's madness haunted her when she closed her eyes. His fists pounding on her body relentlessly. The knife making shallow cuts on her body as if to prolong her torture. He'd tried time and time again to rape her, yet every time he pushed her thighs apart, squeezing the flesh without mercy, his flaccid cock would betray him.

Of course, that only angered him more causing the beatings to begin again. He would leave and return hours later only to start again. Unable to take anymore, she closed her eyes and darkness swept over her again.

When she opened them, it was daylight outside.

Looking around the room, she noticed that for the first time, she was alone. With great effort, she lifted herself up and sat on the edge of the bed. Standing gingerly, she rose to use the bathroom. Surprisingly, she made that little trip without incident and was pretty proud of herself. She washed her hands and face, and noticed a brand-new comb and brush on the vanity with several hair ties and clips, next to a toothbrush and toothpaste, as well as deodorant. She tried to smile, wondering if her dark hero put it there for her.

Grace pulled her hair back in a ponytail, letting her fingers glide gently over the stitches at the top of her forehead. She looked down at the NAVY t-shirt she was wearing, the hem hitting her knees. It had to be his. Turning, she spied a stack of clothing on the end of the bed. She picked up each piece looking at the sizes and once again smiled. Everything looked like it might fit.

She pulled on the clean bra and panties, and then the faded, frayed jeans which fit like a second skin. They brushed slightly against the cuts on her legs, but it wasn't uncomfortable. She then pulled on a white t-shirt with a picture of an old album cover on it. A soft knock at the door made her raise her head.

"Well, hello there, beautiful!" said the cheery voice of her hero. "You look great, and you got up and dressed by yourself. I'd say that's an improvement." Grace could only nod as it still hurt to open her mouth.

"Th-thank you... for... every..." Ghost held up his hand and shook his head.

"It's okay, baby girl. No need to thank us. Are you hungry? We have dinner ready downstairs, and Doc made sure we had some soft foods for you."

Grace gave a short nod and looked down to see his big bear paw reaching for her. She flinched slightly, scolding herself even as she did it. Ghost grimaced.

"I'm sorry, baby girl. I didn't mean to scare you. There's a bunch of folks downstairs, and I just thought you might feel better if we went down together." She nodded and tentatively reached her own fingers toward his. For a big man, Ghost's grip was gentle and consoling. At the door, Grace looked down at her bare feet and shrugged. Quick movements caused instant pain, so she moved carefully and slowly. As they reached the staircase, she stopped, the ascent making her head swim.

"I'm going to pick you up, okay? I won't hurt you. I'll let you down when we get to the kitchen, okay?" he said calmly. Grace nodded once again. Ghost placed one arm behind her knees and the other firmly around her back, his wide, warm hand resting at the curve of her waist.

Fuck, this woman feels good!

"Everyone here is a friend, Grace, everyone. They're all trying to find who did this to you, all of them. And they will all protect you; you don't have anything to fear. Okay?" She gave a simple nod, and he smiled at her.

Grace heard the noise before she saw the massive group of men milling around the tables in the large dining-hall-like kitchen. As Ghost entered the room, he started to let her down, but Grace held tight to his neck.

"It's okay, Grace. I won't let you down." He whispered in her ear as color drained from her face.

"Well, there's the prettiest patient I've ever had," said Doc, moving slowly toward her. "How are you feeling, sweetheart?" She tilted her head slightly sideways and gave a small shrug.

"Are you hungry, beautiful?" asked Tango. Again, she gave a slight shrug, and Tango smiled at her.

Ghost moved toward the big table and set Grace down next to him on the bench. She inched closer to him, and he felt the heat from her side melt against him. She was terrified, and it fucking pissed him off.

"It's okay, Grace. Let me introduce you to everyone, okay?" She nodded and looked down the massive tables. The men were all quiet, smiling tentatively at her, afraid they would scare her. "You already know Doc and Tango. That's Whiskey, Gunner, and Razor. We founded this MC together. We also all served together in the military."

That made sense, thought Grace. The way he referred to them as his brothers and teammates. They also all had the bearing of military men with the badass tattoos and attitude of bikers. It fit.

"Then we have Hawk and his twin Eagle. Eagle's the one who found you at the gate." Grace felt the tears coming and tried to shake them off. "Hey, hey, baby, it's all good. It's okay." Ghost had no idea it wasn't the fact that Eagle found her that had her in tears. It was that he was a twin like her twins.

"Further down, we have Blade, Devil, Zulu, Gunner, Alpha, and Skull. A few of the guys are out on the road working some jobs, and a few others are still in the garage at the front of the property." Grace looked at him questioningly, and he smiled down at her. "We own a garage on-property, but the house and everything are behind the gates. No one can get to you here, Grace. You have free reign of the property, just don't leave outside the gates for now? Okay?"

Grace nodded as Doc set a bowl of soup in front of her with a small pudding cup. She smiled at the man, and he favored her with one in return. The noise picked up a bit, but all of the men were highly respectful of Grace's condition and her skittishness. She noticed the fading evening light, realizing she'd actually woken up in the afternoon, not morning.

As the tables were cleared and the food removed, the five remaining men sat across from her at the table, Ghost still at her side. Tango, Doc, Razor, Whiskey, and Gunner smiled at her.

"Grace, honey, we'd like to ask you some questions. Is that okay?" asked Gunner. Grace nodded, feeling the nervousness and bile rise in her throat.

"Grace, we did some checking to see if we could find out what happened to you. Are you Grace Easton?" asked Gunner. She swallowed and gave a nod. "I see, well then, I'm fucking sorry like you wouldn't believe about your family, Grace."

Grace nodded again and felt the sting of tears. More than two weeks and she was still numb, filled with pain that wouldn't do her the decency of rising up and out of her body.

"Your ex-husband, Kyle Easton, was he the one responsible for what happened to you?" asked Tango. Again, Grace nodded, tears sliding down her beautiful cheeks. Ghost reached out and wiped them away with his napkin, squeezing her fingers gently between his.

"I'm sorry we have to ask these questions, Grace," said Tango. "Were you taken by Kyle?" She nodded. "He beat you?" Again, a nod.

Grace looked out at the darkness and paled. Yes, he beat me; yes, he killed my children and my parents; yes, he stole my life. Stole my soul… YES! She wanted to scream, wanted to run.

Grace stood from the table, and Ghost stood with her. Grace stared into space, her eyes never meeting those of her protectors.

"I think she's had enough for now," he said, glaring at the other men.

She moved toward the door of the kitchen and looked both ways down the hallway, turning right toward the back porch where several other brothers were enjoying the night breeze.

As Grace stepped through the screen door, they stopped their conversation and just smiled at her, but she made no indication of seeing them. Ghost, Gunner, and Tango followed, watching her step off the porch and onto the cool grass. She looked toward the forest, seeing the lighted paths of the running trails, and moved closer and closer.

"Ghost..." said Doc.

"I got her," he said, moving slowly behind her, watching her every move. It looked as though she were just going to stand there, and then suddenly, it was as if she were shot from a cannon. One minute she was there and the next she was off, running barefoot down the trail as fast as her injured body would move.

"Grace! Gracie, baby girl, stop! Gracie!" Ghost yelled after her, but she kept running. She needed to run; run until the pain stopped, run until the hurt went away, run until the death and blood were gone; run! "Grace!"

She tripped, falling to her hands and knees, her breath causing fiery pain to creep into her lungs. Tears blinding her eyes, she stayed scrunched on the pathway, curled into a ball. She felt Ghost lower his body behind her, the warmth of his hand reaching for her. She shook her head, and he pulled back. She felt rather than saw the others behind him. It didn't matter. It didn't matter anymore. And then it happened... her dam burst.

"No..." It was a hoarse whisper at first and then louder and louder. "No! NOOOOOOOOOOOOOO! No... my babies... my daughters... why? WHY?" She let out a cry like a wounded animal, and Ghost could take no more. He pulled her body toward him and sat on the damp earth. Her body curled into him on his lap, her hands fisting his t-shirt. The men behind them stared in pain and anger at the sight of the woman breaking down.

Doc knelt beside them, checking her pulse and looking at her feet to be sure she had no cuts or damage.

"You're going to be okay, baby girl," said Ghost. She shook her head back and forth.

"No... no... I'll never be okay," she said through pain.

"I know it feels that way, Gracie, but I promise it will get better. You know why I can promise that? Because I'm going to be there every step of the way to help you." She just cried, gripping his t-shirt in her fists. One by one, the men behind them moved back toward the house, knowing that Ghost would take care of her.

He sat for more than an hour rocking her, letting her sob, moaning with the physical and emotional pain that only she understood, twisting his shirt, her tears soaking through to his skin. Then she was silent, suddenly eerily quiet. Her breathing was even, and he pulled back, looking down at her peacefully sleeping face. Her lashes still dewy with tears, rested against her cheeks, her nose red and raw. He wasn't sure why he did it, but he kissed her forehead and stood easily with her in his arms.

"I'm going to make it okay, Gracie. You and me, we're going to be okay."

CHAPTER SEVEN

"What are you going to do with her, Ghost?" asked Gunner.

"What? What am I going to do with her? Fuck, Gunner, what do you think? I'm going to help her get well, find the fuck-hole of an ex-husband and kill him. That's what I'm going to do." Ghost shoved his hand through his hair, pacing back and forth in the meeting room. His officers were all staring at him, smiling.

"That's not what Gunner meant Ghost, and you know it," said Doc. "You have feelings for that woman. We can see it. Hell, we all have feelings for her. Not in that way, don't panic. Shit! She's been through more than most of us, and we were in combat! I respect the shit out of her."

"I'm worried about her, okay? I'm worried about her injuries and her safety. That's all." He continued his pacing and then looked up at his friends.

"Fuuuuck..." he drawled out. "What the shit is happening?"

"Well, I'm not that kind of doctor, but I would say you're falling in love," said Doc, smiling at his friend.

"I can't be falling in love with her. I'm too fucking old and broken and... Jesus, what am I going to do?" he asked, plopping in his seat. "I think I am falling in love with her. But who the fuck wouldn't? Christ! She's beautiful, strong, hell!"

"Well, they say the first step is to admit you have a problem," grinned Tango.

"You're such a shithead, you know that, right?" grinned Ghost. "Seriously, what am I going to do? I do have feelings for Grace, but fuck if I know whether or not they're just as her protector. She's so fucking fragile. She's been broken and beaten. I don't want to make it worse."

"Brother, just take it slow," said Razor. "Listen, we're all a little broken and old and fucked up, but you couldn't have predicted this. She's been here almost two months now. Every day she heals a little more on the outside. But it's the inside we have to worry about. Sooner or later, she's going to need to speak to someone professionally. She wanders around this place like a ghost. Maybe that's why you're meant to be together." Razor grinned at his friend and prez.

"I agree with that," said Gunner. "Came home the other night after three a.m. and she was just walking the fucking halls. I asked her if she needed something, and she just shook her head, silent like she does. I asked if I could keep her company, and she nodded. Walked those fucking hallways for an hour before she opened her door and just gave me the hint of a smile. She's so fucking sad it makes me want to kill that fucker even more."

"On that," said Ghost, taking in everything his friend told him, "any information on Kyle?"

"None," said Tango. "Local authorities in their little corner of bumfuck Alabama said they lost his trail. Her coworkers reported her missing a week after she was taken. They assumed she was at home still grieving, which is why they didn't call the authorities sooner. Police found the place where he took Grace, and it was empty, so he clearly got away and was alive, most likely still is. One of Grace's coworkers at the restaurant she managed reported seeing someone meeting his description in the parking lot two weeks ago. He's looking for her."

"Well, he won't fucking find her, not before I find him!" scowled Ghost. "Keep trying to find him. What about the Warriors?"

"Yea, the fucking Warriors," said Razor. "Their prez still wants to meet up here at the barn. They want to send ten guys. Asked if we could make sure we have some club girls here. Told him we don't do club girls, but we have a few hang-arounds that are always willing to help out the boys."

Ghost nodded his head. Fucking Warriors. Not now. Not when he needed to make sure that Grace was safe.

"Fine. Send them a message that we'll pick the date and time. Ten men only and I want every one of our men available. I don't want them all here. I don't want him to know how many we really are." Razor nodded.

"We're still short-staffed on bartenders, so we might need some newbie help that night," said Whiskey.

"We'll figure it out. Alright, meetings adjourned." Ghost stood and followed them out of the room. He opened the steel door separating the bar from the main living quarters and stepped through to see a decent crowd at Club Steel tonight. It wasn't a fucking club; it was a bar, but he let the guys name it what they wanted and Club Steel stuck.

One of the hang-arounds came toward him, and he could feel his stomach bottom out. She was a nice girl but wanted more than he was ever willing to give, and truth be told, his head was swimming with thoughts of his beautiful Gracie.

"Hey, Ghost," she said, smiling up at him. Her perky tits were pushing up out of her tiny tank top, the short cut-off shorts barely covering her ass. "How about I make you feel better, baby? It's been a while." She rubbed her fingers over his dick, and it stirred slightly and then decided to play hide and seek.

"No thanks, not interested," he said, grabbing her wrist.

"Come on, Ghost, you know I can suck your dick like nobody else, baby," she smiled, licking her lips.

"Yea, just like you suck everyone else's dick. Not interested and don't touch me again unless I tell you to." He turned to leave, and she gripped his arm.

"You're a fucking asshole, you know that?! I've fucked and sucked you more than any chick here, and you still won't admit we're good together." She was pissed, and now he was getting pissed.

"We're not good together, Ashley. You're good at sucking cock, and the boys enjoy it. You can continue to do that here at our discretion, or you can walk your ass out of here and find another club that appreciates your dick-sucking abilities. I don't and won't ever again."

"It's Amber, you dick!" Ghost had enough. He was done.

"Out!" He pointed toward the door, his face full of anger.

"Wh-what?" she stumbled moving backwards.

"I said out... get... fucking... out of my club! Now! Don't you ever fucking return!"

She turned, grabbed her purse and stumbled toward the door, all eyes suddenly turned in his direction. Tango grinned as a woman sat on his knee, kissing his neck. Whiskey looked at the retreating ass of Amber or Ashley or whoever the fuck she was and smiled.

Most MCs had club girls who suck or fuck anything right on the floor. At Club Steel they could hang around, but nothing was done on the floor. They had guest rooms through the first steel door, but it took getting through the second steel door to get to their private quarters, and no one except Grace ever saw those quarters.

Ghost turned and went back through the two steel doors, taking the long hallway to the back of the barn. Stepping out onto the porch, he plopped himself into an empty rocker and let out a long breath. He shoved his fingers through his hair and leaned back, letting out another long sigh.

"Should I leave?" asked the sweet voice. He jumped a mile high, gripping his chest.

"Holy fuck! Gracie, no, baby girl, you never have to leave. I mean, no, you don't need to leave. It's just been a long day." He moved to the other side of the porch where she sat on the double swing, her long, lean legs swinging back and forth. "Can I join you?"

Grace nodded and patted the seat next to her. They just sat there swinging for what seemed an hour. Ghost wasn't going to rush her, and truth be told, he was happy as fuck just sitting with her.

"Will you... will you tell me about the club? What do you do here?" she asked tentatively.

"Nothing illegal, Grace, I assure you. Believe me, I know that many clubs get a reputation as being outlaw, but we are not. We own the garage, as you know, and it's quite profitable. Plus, we own the bar at the front of the barn."

"Yea, I sometimes... I hear music and... ummm... I guess the guys bring home guests." She turned toward the dark night, but he could see the blush in her cheeks and cursed. He'd have to ask the guys to be quiet or move Grace further down the hall toward his room, so she would be closer if there was trouble. *Yea, that's why, dickhead.*

"Sorry about that. We're all single and... well..."

"Right, I didn't mean to pry. I mean, you can have anyone you want..."

"Whoa, whoa, I don't bring anyone to my room ever, Gracie. I'm not interested in anyone at the moment. No one, except you." He reached for her fingers and linked his hand gently with hers, hoping she wouldn't pull away. She didn't even look down.

"I'm broken, Ghost. Completely broken." She was so quiet he barely heard her, but he did, and he heard the pain mixed with her words.

"You're not broken, baby girl. You're sad and angry. We all are. But we'll work through that. Together I hope."

"Why are you helping me?" she asked quietly, turning to stare at him with those green eyes that invaded his dreams every night.

"Why? Fucking hell, Grace, because you need us and I think we... I might need you. You showed up on our doorstep beaten within an inch of your life, but so fucking beautiful my hard heart cracked. I looked at you and knew I would hunt down the bastard that hurt you." She waited patiently, saying nothing.

"We do this for a living, Grace. My brothers and I, we're all former military. I told you that once, but you might have been out of it." Grace searched the memories and felt like she found the one he referred to. "We take on cases, missions that others won't. Lost children, human trafficking, slumlords, that kind of thing. We help those that can't help themselves."

Grace nodded and turned to look at him, look in his eyes. He had the bluest eyes she'd ever seen. His hair was dark but laced with fine strands of silver, his long beard wrapped around the most luscious lips.

"My daughters couldn't help themselves. All they wanted to do was celebrate their graduation with my parents and their friends. All they wanted to do was go off to Europe for the trip we'd all saved for. All they wanted to do was go off to college, get married, and have ba... babies..." Her voice cracked, and Ghost pulled her closer, her head resting on his shoulder.

"I know, baby girl; I know, and I'm so fucking sorry they won't get to do those things."

"When will it stop hurting, Ghost? When?" she cried.

"I don't know, honey. I know that I've lost brothers in war, and I can tell you I still think about them and feel their deaths. They weren't blood-related, so I can only imagine what you're feeling. I think when you're ready, Grace, you need to talk to someone... professionally."

"I don't want to leave the property... I can't," she whispered.

"I know, baby girl. We'll figure it out. Will you tell me about your daughters?" he asked. She was quiet for the longest time, and he'd nearly given up hope when she started to speak.

"I was shocked when I learned I was having twins. It didn't run in my family or Kyle's, so I was terrified. The first few years were okay, but he kept losing his job... getting fired. I had a degree in business, so it was easier for me. I managed a local restaurant – everything, top to bottom and really loved it. I was able to work around the girls' school schedules, attend their events, things like that.

"Anyway, then I found out he got fired for screwing the receptionist in a supply closet. I was done. I filed for divorce and full custody and was granted it. A year later, he started making threats and coming to the house, always angry at me about something, trying to hit me."

Ghost gripped the back of the swing so hard he thought it might crack. He was fucking angry, but he didn't want to show that to Grace right now.

"I was granted a restraining order and for the most part, he abided by it. The day..." she swallowed, and he rubbed her back slowly. "The day of the party, I left to pick up the cake, and he called saying he wanted permission to come to the party. The girls didn't want him there, so I said no. He said, 'then this is your fault,' he said it was my fault, and he was right."

"No. No fucking way is this your fault, baby girl, and you need to get rid of those thoughts. This was on him. He did this. If you had been there, he'd have killed you too."

"I know you're right. In my head, I know you're right. My heart just doesn't feel it yet. Anyway, after the the worst church service of my life, I buried both daughters and my parents on the same day. After, I went home and locked myself in with a bottle of Jameson. That's the last I remember until I woke up in that room... beaten... beaten..." She sniffed, and Ghost pulled her closer still.

"Faith and Hope. They were so beautiful, Ghost, so damned beautiful and smart. When I see Eagle and Hawk, it reminds me of what I've lost. The girls," she laughed through her tears, " the girls would have thought they were cute. Both had scholarships to university. Hope was going to be a nurse, and Faith was studying engineering. My girls..." she hiccupped a sob and settled herself once again, "... my girls had their whole lives... it's not fair... it's..."

"I know, baby girl. I know," he said, holding her tighter. He pulled Grace further to him, settling her on his lap as she wrapped her arms around his neck. "I wish I could take it all away, Gracie, every fucking speck of bad. I wish I could take it. I can't, but if you let me, Grace, if you just give me a chance, baby girl, I want to make it better for you in other ways."

Grace sobbed against his neck, her warm breath and salty tears staining his skin. He just continued to rub her back until she settled. When she finally looked up into his face, one small, slender hand cupped his jaw, turning his face slightly toward her.

"You're such a good man, Ghost, such a good and decent man." She rubbed her hand along his jaw and smiled. "I like the beard, Ghost. It suits you." He smiled at her, just waiting. He would not push this woman and definitely would not cause her more pain.

"I want to let you try, Ghost. I like you, probably more than like you, but I'm such a mess."

"You're not a mess, baby girl. You're beautiful and strong and hurt."

"Will you kiss me?" she asked against his mouth. The warm breath of her words touched his lips, and he lifted her easily, his huge hands gripping her waist, turning her to straddle his big legs. Grace settled against his thighs, warmth flooding her core as he slowly leaned forward, his mouth covering hers with silky touches. She melted against him, tasting him.

"You're so fucking beautiful, Gracie. So, fucking perfect, baby girl," he said, sliding his hand into her hair, tugging gently backwards to run his tongue along her neck and throat. "I'm going to make this better for you, baby girl." She nodded.

"You already have, Ghost."

"Eric. My name is Eric Stanton. Ghost was my team name. I was a SEAL, and they used to tease me that I was always hard to find, hard to see for being such a big man. I mean, I'm six-foot-four and two hundred plus, so you'd think they could easily spot me, but anyway. When it's just you and me... Eric..."

"Eric," she said in throaty whisper. "You already have made it better, Eric. Just by being here with me. You have no idea how your gentle touch, your voice has helped me through the darkest days."

"Tomorrow, I want to move you closer to my room. The one next to me is empty, and it's not as noisy down there. You'll be closer to me." She smiled down at him and nodded. "I'm building a house on the property, baby girl. I... Grace, I'd sure like for you to think about moving in with me when the time comes."

Grace leaned her head against his shoulder and let out a long sigh.

"Oh, Eric, I want so badly to say yes, but there's so much I need to work through first. Can you let me figure all this out first? Please?"

"I will wait forever for you, baby girl, forever, because you are so fucking worth it."

"Is there… is there something I could do… a job… around here? Is there a job around here I could do?" she asked tentatively.

"A job? Baby girl, you don't need a job."

"I do need a job, Eric. I need to feel useful again. I need to not have so much time on my hands to think about other stuff. I can do anything. Cook, dishes, laundry, something!"

"Well, I don't know. We've been looking for a bartender but…"

"I'll take it!" she said, jumping from his lap.

"Whoa, whoa, whoa," he said, smiling at her. "Baby girl, I love that you want to do something with us, but bartending at the club bar isn't easy. I mean, these guys are nice when you see them day-to-day, but in the club, well, in the club it can get raunchy. We have outside patrons who know this is an MC bar and fights break out pretty regularly. Some of the girls…"

"The club sluts."

"The what? Who the fuck…?" his eyes got big as saucers as he looked at his sweet Gracie.

"I overheard the guys talking. The club sluts or, ummm… hang-arounds that was it, they offer to service the guys for free. I get it. I'm not so old that I don't understand how it works."

"Baby girl, you're not old at all. Wait, how old are you?" he asked, looking down at her sweet face.

"I'm forty-one. How old are you?" she smiled. It was a smile. The first genuine smile he'd seen since her arrival.

"I'm forty-six. Look, baby, if you want to try, we'll try, but it gets rough out there. The bar fights can get crazy, and the girls, well, they're just…"

"Do you, ummm, you do the girls? I mean, go off with the girls?" she asked.

"I won't lie to you, Gracie. I've been with a few, but always protected and never all night. I'm a man, and I have needs, but I never lied to one of them about what I wanted, and it was always only one time and just sex. I just haven't dated in a really long time, and these aren't the girls I would date. They serve a…"

"… a purpose," she said, grinning at him. He nodded. "Well then, give me a trial. I'll bartend a few nights, and you let me know how I do. If I'm good, then I get a job. If I'm not, well then, I guess, I'll have to figure out something else to help you with." She stood on her toes and kissed him again, only this time it wasn't timid or unsure. It was filled with warmth and desire.

It was ten minutes later before Ghost's brain kicked in and realized he was standing alone on the porch, in the dark, with a raging hard-on.

CHAPTER EIGHT

She had a job, a real job where she'd earn money and be able to support herself. She could pay back the club for all they've done for her and maybe buy a secondhand car. She wouldn't have to rely on Ghost for everything. She loved living at the barn with the guys, but sooner or later, they were going to want her out. She was certain her presence was definitely cramping their style.

Ghost, true to his word, moved her to the room closest to him, which turned out to be twice the size of the other guest room. She had a small sitting area with a comfortable loveseat, a good-sized flat screen television, a large bathroom, and walk-in closet.

After the first week, she wondered if Ghost had cameras in her room because every morning as she opened her door to head down for breakfast, he'd open his at the same time. They hadn't kissed since the night on the porch other than a quick peck here or there, but whenever she saw him, her face would flood with heat, and her panties would flame with desire.

She'd cursed herself for that on more than one occasion. How could she be thinking about Ghost in that way when she was still grieving the death of her family? *How could I so selfishly want a happily ever after?*

Because you're human, Gracie, and you deserve something good.

Grace looked in the mirror once more and smiled. Her dark hair was pulled high on her head in a messy bun, fine strands framing her face. It was a face not quite her own yet. The broken nose changed the way she looked, and the swelling in her cheeks was still present, making her more cherubic than lean. She had a light coat of mascara on her lashes and a pale pink gloss on her lips.

The dark-washed jeans clung low to her hips, and the red tank top covered her breasts but gave just a glimpse of her average cleavage. On her feet, she wore a comfortable pair of cowboy boots. Around her neck were several loose chains and at her wrists, several wrap-leather bracelets.

Poor Doc had volunteered to take her shopping a few days ago, and Grace was certain he regretted it. Three hours of moving through the mall and he looked positively miserable, but he never said a word. He followed her, dutifully carrying her bags, and escorted her back home safely.

"Okay, you can do this," she whispered to herself. She opened her door and headed down the long hallway, taking the steps to the main floor. As she went to open the second steel door, Gunner came out of the meeting room.

"Whoa! Grace, you look fucking amazing!" he smiled down at her, and Grace laughed.

"Thanks, Gunner."

"No, seriously, shit, ummm, has Ghost seen you yet?"

"N-no, why? Is this not okay to tend bar? Do I need a uniform or something?" she asked innocently.

"Uh, no – no uniform, it's just, well, he did explain that the crowd can get rowdy, right, hun?"

"He did," she said, smiling up at him. "It's okay, Gunner, really. Listen, I r-raised two teenaged girls…" She wiped away a tear and then felt pride in herself that she didn't completely break down, "I raised two teenaged girls, and I managed a restaurant for years. I'll be okay. You'll be in there, right?"

"I'll be there, sweetie."

He opened the door and watched as all eyes turned toward Grace. She smiled, raising her hand slightly toward the guys, all sitting at a large round table, who all grinned at her and then turned to look at the open-jawed shock of Ghost.

Grace pretty much wore the same thing every day since she'd arrived. Jeans, t-shirts, no shoes, and hair in a ponytail, with no makeup. Seeing her put some effort into her appearance was a shock to them all, but no one more so than Ghost.

"Hi, Eagle," she said sweetly, "I'm here to take over for you."

"Hi, Grace, you look beautiful, by the way," he said, smiling at the older woman.

"Thank you, and I-I never got to say thank you for rescuing me, Eagle." She reached for his arm and squeezed. He was in his early twenties, but he was tall and muscular, dark blonde hair with crystal blue eyes just like his twin. "It was... it was everything to me."

"I'm happy I was there, Grace. I'll be hanging out if it gets too bad, but it should be okay tonight. It's Wednesday."

"Eagle? I also wanted to tell you sometimes I look at you and Hawk... I... get emotional..." He reached over and touched her hand, smiling.

"I know Gracie. We're twins. I sure wish we'd have met your girls. If they were as beautiful as their momma, well, you'd have twin sons-in-law." He winked at her, and she smiled, a small flutter in her stomach.

You're going to be okay.

She nodded and stood behind the bar, wiping the bar top off. She heard someone sit on a stool and looked up to see Ghost.

"What can I get... Ghost..." she smiled at him. His face was serious, filled with concern and something she couldn't quite put her finger on. "Are you okay?"

"Yea, yea, you just... you look fucking beautiful, baby girl. Fucking hot as fuck!" Grace laughed a soft, lilting laugh and reached across to grab his hand.

"Thank you, Ghost, Eric, thank you."

"I just... if anyone bothers you, baby..."

"It's going to be okay. I promise. Can I... um... can I get a kiss for good luck?" she asked, blushing from her chest to her brow.

"Every fucking second of the day, baby." He leaned over the bar, his tall body reaching her easily, and kissed her softly, at first, until she gripped the back of his head and slid her tongue between his lips. She lingered, tasting him, beer and burger and man. Then pulled back, realizing the entire bar was staring at them.

"Maybe tonight, maybe you should, maybe, ummm, watch a movie with me or something in my room?" He nodded but could say nothing else as she moved to the other end of the bar and poured a beer. He didn't even remember making his way back to the table, but he damned sure remembered his teammates teasing him. Forty-six years old, and he was being teased like some horny high school kid.

Grace couldn't help but watch Ghost with his friends. He was so damned handsome and strong. She'd never met a man like him in her entire life. Of course, Kyle was her first, and she didn't date while raising the girls, so there wasn't much to judge him by. But damn! He was making her think thoughts that only her raunchy romance novels talked about.

She'd dreamt of those arms wrapped around her, those big legs holding her down, his rough hands squeezing her breasts, and, yes, she'd seen the outline of his cock on more than one occasion and dreamt of that as well.

Grace's thoughts were brought back to the present as the bar picked up. It was busy, steady streams of people coming and going. She noticed a few of the hang-arounds and how skimpy they dressed, and she also noticed that they were more than willing to do just about anything for the guys, although Ghost had a rule – no sex in the club. But she noticed more than one head back to the private rooms.

Around midnight, things really started to pick up. Two guys playing pool began arguing over who was the winner, while a girl rubbed on Eagle, only for another girl to come over and pull her hair, calling her every name in the book. Ghost watched it all but didn't interfere.

When the arguments in both directions started to get heated, it was all Grace could handle. As a mother, she'd stepped in on more than a few arguments with her girls or their friends. She'd coached several of their athletic teams and had to maneuver the dangerous grounds of female emotions. Stepping from behind the bar, she stormed toward the pool tables.

"Brother," said Gunner, nudging Ghost. "Brother! You might want to check out your woman."

"Oh fuck!"

Ghost tried to push through the crowds to the back of the club where the pool tables were. When he finally got there, the crowd parted, and there was silence except for the voice of one furious little mama.

"... and you! She wouldn't be calling you a slut monkey if you'd dress more like a young woman. You can still show all your assets without looking like you belong on a street corner. Clean up your shit, dress for respect AND sex, and you won't get names thrown at you. And you!" she said, pointing to the other girl. "Don't throw stones at glasshouses. You don't look much different. If you don't like the look, change it, but don't bring your shit in here!"

"You two," she said, pointing at the guys at the pool table who jumped back as if she would strike them, "if you can't play a decent game, get the fuck out of this bar! We don't allow fights here, and I don't need your childish behavior. Straighten up!" Both men stood straighter and swallowed, watching the tiny woman tear into them.

"Now, show's over. Stop with your shit and enjoy your Wednesday night." Grace turned to head back behind the bar when a thunderous roar of applause went up. She looked around, trying to see what they were cheering about.

"That's for you, baby girl, all for you," said Ghost, kissing her. "I've never seen anything so damned hot in all my life. You are amazing!"

Grace felt the adrenaline pumping and smiled up at him. She looked over at Eagle, and he grinned.

"Eagle? Can you take over the bar?" He nodded at her as she grabbed Ghost's hand and moved toward the steel door.

"Where are we going, baby girl?" he asked, grinning at her.

"To fix a problem."

CHAPTER NINE

"What problem are we fixing, baby?" asked Ghost as they stepped inside her room.

"Mine. I need you, Ghost. I need to feel your body, to touch your body. I've been dancing around this for weeks and..."

She didn't get another word out before his lips crashed against hers. Grace was already pulling on his t-shirt, yanking it over his head. She pulled her own tank top off and quickly unhooked the bra, letting it fall to the floor.

Ghost broke free of her lips to remove his boots and undid his belt buckle. She did the same, sliding her jeans off. Standing in only her panties, he licked his lips and moved toward her.

"Please, Eric, I need you," she whimpered.

"Baby girl, I need you too, but I don't want to hurt you. I want to savor you, take my time with you, taste you," he said, sliding his fingers into the waistband of her panties. He pulled them down, kneeling as he did. He stayed there, smelling her sex, his nose buried in her dark curls. As he pushed her backwards on the bed, she tried to scoot back, and he shook his head, pulling her forward to the edge.

"No, baby, I wanna taste you. I need to taste you, Gracie," he whispered against her soft hair.

Grace moaned and spread her legs wide for him as he ran his gentle fingers inside her thighs. For just a moment, Grace had a flash of fear remembering Kyle and his hands on her thighs, but it was gone in a moment, replaced by the gentle giant of a man between her legs.

His warm breath made her arch her back. He slid his hand up her belly and pushed her down, his tongue flicking against her sex as she sucked in a breath. Sliding one finger inside her, she moaned again.

"Oh shit! Eric… Eric, please, baby…"

"Sssshhhh," he hushed her, "let me take my time, woman."

She laughed, and he couldn't help but smile. Fucking hell, this woman tasted so good. His tongue ran up and down her slit, his finger moving in and out while she writhed against the bed. Ghost pulled his finger out and then slid two into her tight channel.

"Fuck, baby girl, you're so tight," he said, licking her. "I feel you, baby. Let yourself go for me."

"Eric… Eric, please… I need to…"

"Let go, baby girl," he said, diving into her slit with his tongue.

She cried out, gripping his hair, holding him in place. Grace's body shuddered against his face, her hands frantically grasping his hair, pulling him toward her. She covered his mouth with hers, tasting her juices on his tongue, feeling her wetness in his beard.

"I need you, Gracie. Let me get a condom, baby."

"No, I can't have any more children. I want to feel you, Eric, please."

"Fuck, baby, yea, that's perfect. I wanna feel you too." He stood, and she could see the outline of his erection, massive in his jeans. He slid the jeans down, bending forward, then his boxers. His cock jutted forward and out, so heavy it couldn't stand upright. Grace gasped.

"I-I don't think that's going to fit," she said, reaching for him.

"It will fit, baby girl. You were made me for me, Gracie, just you," he said, crawling toward her, positioning himself between her knees. He pushed her knees wide and then toward her head, touching the tip of his cock to her opening. He moved slowly, letting her take an inch at a time.

"Fuck, baby, why are you so fucking tight?"

"No one... no one since the divorce..." she said, trying to catch her breath.

"Shit! Fuck, baby... oh fuck, Gracie... you're so fucking perfect, baby girl," he said, leaning forward to kiss her. He balanced himself on his elbows and slid in another inch, out and then in another inch, and another...

"Eric, please, I need all of you, now, baby... hard!" She needed him so desperately, wanting to feel every inch of his manhood and every ounce of his sex.

"Shit!" he yelled. Slamming forward he filled her completely, his cock seemingly growing more inside her, filling her more. "Breathe, baby... breathe..."

Grace cupped his face and pulled him toward her kissing him, tasting him. She rocked her hips forward, feeling his huge cock stretch her body, filling her. She took a fistful of his hair and pulled him closer. Ghost grinned down at the tiny woman, pumping harder.

"Yes, yes, that's it. Right there... oh God! Eric, that's it, more!"

"You're mine, Gracie. You hear me, baby girl? You're fucking mine!"

"Yours... fuck me...fuck me!" she screamed as he pumped furiously inside her. "Eric, I'm coming!"

Those words from her lips were all he needed. He slammed into the racking shudders of her body and felt the lava hot juices fill her completely. He'd never had such an intense orgasm in all his forty-six years. He couldn't stop pumping, emptying his dick inside this woman.

"Baby girl… Christ, Gracie! I'm so fucking crazy about you!"

"I'm crazy about you too, Eric. I think I'm falling in love with you," she whispered.

"You think so, huh?" he said, smiling down at her. "Well, good news, Gracie. I fucking love you too." He kissed her sweetly, pulling her body into his arms and enveloping her in his love and protection.

"It all happened so fast," she said in a whisper. "I feel so confused. I'm so happy I found you, but feel so guilty…"

"Baby, baby, your daughters, your parents, I'm sure they would want nothing more than for you to be happy, baby girl. And this is not fast, baby girl. It's love. It happens in its own time. But don't distract me. I was going to spank that ass of yours for putting yourself in harm's way tonight."

"I-I didn't put myself in harm's way!" she said in a huff.

"You did, baby girl. You don't know those hang-around girls like I do. They're dirty, and they fight dirty. And those guys, they weren't our guys, so I don't know how they feel about hitting a woman. I'd hate to have to kill someone in my own club."

"I'm sorry, Eric, but I just couldn't stand there and listen to the juvenile behavior."

"I know, baby, but next time get one of us, okay?" She nodded. "Baby girl, let me hear you say it, or I will follow through on the spanking." She pulled back and stared down at him, smiling.

"Maybe I want the spanking. Did you ever think about..." *Whack!* Grace jumped, shocked by the sudden sting on her ass cheek, then smiled down at Eric. "I think I like that."

"Fuuuuuccckkkk!"

CHAPTER TEN

Grace woke to an empty bed, the sun high in the sky. She smiled as she stretched, and her body moaned from the previous night. For the first time in weeks, it wasn't sore from her attack. It was sore from the intense lovemaking between her and Ghost.

She felt the flashes of shame and sadness once again and quickly dismissed them. She knew that she had to move forward, not back, but she wanted to do that here, not somewhere else. More than anything, she trusted that these men would follow through on their promise to find Kyle. Still, she needed to make sure that they were all on board with her staying for a while and, more than anything, that she expressed herself clearly to Ghost. She wanted no misunderstandings between the two of them ever.

A hot shower washed away the pleasures of the night before, and Grace smiled, feeling happier than she had in many years. Drying her hair, she left it down around her shoulders and pulled on a pair of soft cotton shorts with a blue tank top. She slid her feet into the comfortable running shoes she'd bought with Doc and headed downstairs.

As she reached the kitchen, she heard the loud voices of all the men and stopped at the door, staring at them. She watched as Eagle and Hawk teased one another, and as always, the pang of emptiness hit her, but only briefly before she took joy in the brotherly love they were displaying that only she could see. She then watched as the man she now knew as Zulu stole the orange juice of Tango. He looked up, caught in the act, and smiled.

"Are you going to make me go off on you, Zulu?" she said. The room fell silent in surprise, and she smiled at them all.

"No, ma'am," he said, grinning, "I want no part of the mama bear I saw last night." The room laughed, and Ghost started to rise, but she held her hand out to tell him to sit.

"I-I'd like to talk to all of you for a moment." No one moved, no one said anything, and if he were honest, Ghost was panicked that she might decide to leave.

"I've been here almost three months now. Through the entire summer. Can you believe it?" She laughed, not expecting an answer from any of them. "I loved bartending last night, and if I've passed the test, I'd like to continue to take shifts doing that. I felt useful.

"But what I really want to say to all of you is thank you. From the moment I fell into Eagle's arms, you all have welcomed me and made me feel as though I'm part of the family."

"You are part of the family, Gracie," said Doc.

"Doc, sweet Doc, you have no idea how much I appreciate your stellar care during all of this. If it wasn't you, it was Tango or Ghost at my bedside talking to me, holding my hand. My physical well-being is good, but I know you all know this. I need the inside to get well also. I want to find a therapist. If possible, someone that could come here."

"I can find someone for you, Gracie," said Doc, smiling at her.

"Okay, good, that's good. I also... I also know that I'm cramping your style big time by being here."

"What the fuck are you talking about, Grace?" asked Tango. "You're not cramping anyone's style, honey. We love having you here."

"But... but the girls..."

"There are no girls we want to bring to our rooms, Grace," said Gunner. "If we take a girl, it's in the guestrooms downstairs. We want you here, Grace." She let out a long sigh of relief, and Ghost watched her, his chest constricted tight.

"Okay, well then, I'd like to stay a while longer. If I'm honest, it's two-fold. I'm terrified that Kyle will find me. I hate that the most. That he stole my feeling of independence and freedom. I have nightmares about him... about..." She trailed off, catching her breath, and Ghost's heart broke into a thousand pieces.

"He won't get to you here, Gracie," said Hawk.

"I know, sweet boy," she said, smiling at the young man. Hawk and Eagle were twenty-three years old, but to her, they were boys. "I just can't logically think past those gates right now."

"What's your second reason, Grace?" asked Razor.

"Well, I'd like to stay with Ghost. Because of Ghost, if he'll have me." She walked toward him, standing between his opened knees, and placed her hands on either side of his head. "I want to stay, Ghost, with you. I'm so messed up... so... I don't even know what I am anymore, but I want to see what happens. Can we do that?"

"Baby girl, we are so doing that!" he stood, lifting her with him, kissing her in front of the entire team. Cheers rose from the group, and Grace blushed, smiling into his shoulder. "I love you, baby girl."

"I love you, Ghost." Grace held tight to his shoulders, her feet lifted off the ground as the men all smiled and cheered for them. When he finally set her down, they were both smiling ear to ear.

"Hungry, baby?" he asked.

"After last night, I'm starving," she smiled with a blush. Ghost laughed and pulled her toward the table where she dug into the huge breakfast that George fixed.

George was an older African American man who she now knew served in Vietnam. He'd been evicted from his home, unable to pay the mortgage, and came to the boys for help. Six years later, he was living in the largest of the downstairs rooms, doing something he loved, cooking for men he loved and respected.

"George, this is delicious!" she said, smiling at the man.

"Thank you, Gracie. It's nice to know someone in this place has decent manners and appreciates hard work."

"Oh, come on, George," said Gunner, "you know we all appreciate you, brother." He winked at Grace, and she smiled inwardly.

"So," she started, "can I keep bartending a few nights a week?" She looked around the room. Tango stood up and spoke first.

"I say yes, but, and it's a big but, Gracie girl, no more going off like you did last night. I don't give a fuck if you hurt anyone's feelings. I was worried they might hurt you."

"Yea, Mr. tall dark and serious said the same thing," she said, nodding at Ghost. The men all laughed at her description of him, and he frowned in a playful way.

"We just don't want you hurt, Gracie," said Zulu.

He was a strikingly beautiful man. Easily an inch or two taller than Ghost, his muscles were thick, rippling beneath his t-shirt. His head was shaved, his cocoa-colored skin glowing in the morning light. He had full, thick lips that most women would die for.

"Thank you, Zulu. But if all of you are here, won't I be safe?" she asked it both as a statement and question. In truth, she'd put her entire trust into the fact that she would be safe with all of them here.

"In theory, yes," said Ghost, "but we all know that things can go sideways fast. If one of those men had a gun, or if one of the girls had a knife…"

"I get it," she said, holding up a hand, suddenly feeling a bit nauseous. "Okay, no more mama bear routines without some backup." Ghost nodded for now. Eventually, he didn't want her to do shit except be his woman, but he knew that she needed this for now.

Tango's phone rang, and as he answered it, the others began talking again. He whispered something to Eagle and Hawk, who stood and looked down the table at Grace.

"Hey, Grace," said Hawk, "how about we show you the inventory, how to connect the kegs, stuff like that?"

"Sure!" she said excitedly, standing from her seat. She kissed Ghost, and the twins moved with her, one in front, one in back, and nodded at the room.

"What's up?" asked Zulu.

"Someone's at the garage saying that their SUV was found in the county impound lot. Claims it was his wife's vehicle, and he needs to find her. She's sick."

"Motherfucker!"

CHAPTER ELEVEN

Skull and Devil were at the garage on the early morning shift trying to finish a bike for a client. It was a custom build with a lot of moving parts, literally, but also a custom paint job. Skull was the expert artist on the paint, and he'd done a fantastic job on the tank of the bike. The design of a scene important to the buyer showed the Grand Canyon in almost 3-D on the tank. They hoped that this would be the one to really highlight their skills and put them on the map.

Gunner heard the bell above the door in the reception area and wiped his hands on the rag hanging from his pocket. He opened the door to the air-conditioned space and sucked in the cool air hitting his face. A pale man in his forties stared at him, his unkempt thinning hair flying everywhere.

"Can I help you?" asked Gunner.

"Yea, I... my wife is missing. She's sick, like sick in the head. I found her SUV at the impound lot." Gunner eyed the man and immediately knew who this guy was most likely.

"And? If you found the SUV, then why are you here?" asked Gunner. He reached over to the speaker system leading to the garage and flipped the switch so that Skull and Devil would hear the conversation.

"The sheriff said it was found about fifteen miles from here. I'm just asking all the businesses in the area if they've seen this woman," he said, pushing a photo toward Gunner. Gunner recognized a much younger Grace but didn't give away anything.

"She's awfully young," he said casually.

"Oh, well, that's an older picture. Have you seen her?" he asked again.

"Nope. We're a motorcycle club. No women allowed on premises unless they're here for our entertainment, if you know what I mean," said Gunner, trying to smile. He noticed the lifted brows and immediate curiosity of the man in front of him. Sick son-of-a-bitch.

"Really? Well, ummm, maybe some other time…"

"I thought you were looking for your wife. You telling me you're interested in fucking some biker chicks when you have that at home?" he said, no longer smiling at the man.

"No! No, that's not what I meant." Sweat was pouring down the face of Kyle Easton, and Gunner was enjoying this more than he could possibly say. This prick hurt their Gracie girl, and he didn't have a fucking clue what he just walked into. Gunner could only smile as he saw the images of Ghost, Tango, Zulu, and Gunner coming through the garage.

The door opened, and the warm breezes from outside filled the small space as the four men walked into the reception area. Kyle looked up at the large men and started to back toward the door.

"Where you goin', friend?" asked Ghost. "I understand you're looking for a woman?"

"No, I've made a mistake… I…" he turned faster than anyone thought he could and was out the door in his vehicle before they could stop him. He locked the doors and sped from the gravel parking lot, turning back towards the small mountain town.

"Find him!" yelled Ghost. Zulu and Gunner headed toward their bikes and took off after him. "I want that son-of-a-bitch in my hands by the end of the week."

Ghost paced back and forth in the lobby of the garage, running his hands through his hair, tugging at his beard in frustration. He would not let this man touch Grace ever again. What kind of sick fuck kills his own children? He would not let this demon live to kill again.

"Ghost! Ghost!" yelled Gunner. "You've got to calm down, brother. You're going to have a heart attack." Ghost stared at his teammate and friend. Gunner was younger than Ghost, but only by a few years. At thirty-seven, he'd retired from the Army and sought a place to feel the brotherhood once more just like the others.

Comment [MK]: I changed this because I realized Gunner was in the original group.

"I can't calm down. I can't let Gracie down. I can't..." the emotions overwhelmed him, and he sat in one of the hard plastic chairs in the reception area, his head in his hands. Tango sat next to him and nudged him, smiling.

"Brother, listen to me. We will get this prick. All you need to do is worry about that beautiful woman back there in the house waiting on you. That's it. Just you and her. Trust us in this. We will find him, and he will die by your hand."

Ghost nodded and stood, gripping Tango's shoulder in a brotherly squeeze. Tango watched as his friend went through the gate and followed the gravel path back toward the barn.

"Damn! He's got it bad, doesn't he?" said Skull. Tango smiled and turned toward his friend.

"No, brother, he's got it good. We should all be so fucking lucky."

CHAPTER TWELVE

"So, if you need a keg changed, just ask one of us or any of the guys in the bar. Everyone knows how to do it. The deliveries are made once a month unless we need them sooner, but we take care of that, you won't have to deal with the delivery drivers. Liquor is ordered from a vendor via a form online, and it's shipped to us, again once a month," said Eagle, smiling down at Grace. She nodded, looking at the shelves piled high with liquor bottles and bottled beer.

"Straws, napkins, all of that is kept here. We don't keep a lot of fruit on hand because, well, honestly, most of the people we get in here want beer or whiskey. If you feel like we're running low on fruit, one of us can always run to the market and pick it up. As you know, we only do minimal bar food. Fries, burgers, pizzas, simple stuff, but you won't ever have to worry about that. Our busy season is actually summer, although we get a good bit in the winter if people come up to ski on the smaller slopes."

They continued to walk along the long shelves, taking their time as Eagle and Hawk wanted to be sure that Grace was out of sight for the time being.

"Will you tell me about you?" asked Grace, smiling at the young men. They were both so handsome. Tall, muscular, dark blonde hair and blue eyes; they were strikingly good looking, and even at forty-one, she noticed that.

"Not much to tell, Gracie," said Hawk, smiling down at her. She waited patiently, making him shift from one foot to the other uncomfortably. "Okay, so here's the short version. We graduated from high school, but our grades weren't good enough for college. Decided we'd join the Marines and see what the world had to offer. We both stayed four years."

"And what did you do in the Marines?" she asked.

"Snipers. We were both snipers. It's how we got our names Eagle and Hawk. They couldn't name us the same thing, so they came up with those names. We're both blessed with great vision, better than great in fact, and had a lot of credited kills. I mean..." She smiled, holding up her hand and nodded. She understood what they were saying.

"I like those names," she said, smiling. "They seem to fit. You're both always watching, always looking, like an Eagle or a Hawk. Will you tell me your real names?"

"Grace, if you haven't figured it out yet, we can't refuse you anything," said Hawk, smiling. "My name is Ryan, and he's Tyran, or Ry and Ty, whatever you like, beautiful."

"I like those names. Ry and Ty. They fit you both as well. My girls, Hope and Faith, they were beautiful girls, long honey-blonde hair, green eyes, and so smart." She looked toward the door, a tear coming down her cheek.

"You don't have to talk about them If you don't want to, Grace." Hawk reached for her hand, but she only smiled and looked at the two identical men.

"No. No, I've found that it helps, actually. They would have loved the two of you," she said, laughing. "They always said they wanted to marry twins because only twins would understand what it's like to be a twin." They both shook their heads and smiled.

"We're glad you're here, Gracie girl," said Eagle. "We're not happy about how you got here, never wish that on anybody, but we're damn sure happy you're here." She nodded again, smiling at both men.

"So, you were both snipers? Good with guns?" she asked. Hawk eyed the little woman and nodded. "Would you... would you teach me how to use a weapon?" Eagle stepped back quickly as if she'd scalded his skin.

"I don't know, Grace. I think you need to talk to Ghost about that."

"Talk to Ghost about what?" came the booming voice behind them. He looked at both young men and back towards Grace. "Talk to Ghost about what?" he asked more insistently.

"I want to learn to use a gun," she said calmly. Ghost walked toward her smiling. His hands framed her face and kissed her sweetly.

"I love you, baby girl, but hell to the fucking no!"

CHAPTER THIRTEEN

"Ghost! Ghost, wait up!" she yelled at his retreating back. He pounded through the steel door into the club. A few patrons were enjoying an early lunch, and he smiled in their direction as they stared at the menacing-looking man with the beautiful woman following him, but he didn't slow his steps. Grace picked up the pace, following more quickly.

"Ghost, please…" It was the 'please' that got to him. Damned if he could refuse this woman anything. He stopped and turned, pulling her into his arms, wrapping those big muscular arms around her body, squeezing.

"Baby girl, I cannot lose you," he whispered against her hair. He was holding her so tightly; Grace couldn't catch her breath. Finally pushing away enough to look up at him, she touched his face sweetly.

"Ghost, teaching me to defend myself is not going to make you lose me. I want to learn. I need to – for me. Please," she pleaded. He held her against his chest, reigning kisses down across her head, down her forehead and her cheeks.

It was selfish, really. If he didn't teach her, it would be one more reason that she needed him, that she'd want to stay for his protection. He could have kicked his own ass in that moment. It was beyond selfish. She needed to find ways to feel more independent, and if knowing how to use a weapon was one of those ways, then he was going to give it to her.

"Okay."

"Okay?" she asked suspiciously.

"Okay," he smiled, kissing her. "I'll teach you. Not Hawk or Eagle. A handgun only for now."
She nodded, hugging him again, pressing her warm cheek against his chest. He grabbed her hand,

pulling her toward a table reserved for him and the team. Tango, Gunner, and Zulu were already seated with three large pizzas on the table. She sensed that they wanted to talk to her about something, and she wondered if they overheard the conversation about teaching her to use a weapon.

"Baby girl," he said, sitting down with her, "we need to tell you something." Grace stopped mid-bite and stared up at the men. Oh God! They were going to make her leave. They were mad about something; she'd done something wrong.

"Gracie, honey, look at us," said Tango. "You've done nothing wrong." It was as if Tango could read every expression, every thought flitting through her mind and across her face. She let out a whoosh of breath in relief and stared back up at the table of men.

"Baby girl, Kyle came to the garage this morning," said Ghost. He waited for her reaction, wondering how she would take the news. Her body started to shiver as if cold, and he pulled his leather kutte from his body and draped it over her own. The smell of leather and Ghost enveloped her.

"Did he… does he know…"

"He doesn't know you're here, Gracie girl," said Zulu. "He found your car in the sheriff's impound lot. Told them you were his wife, and you were missing. They told him the truth. They knew nothing of a woman matching your description in the area. He got spooked when we started questioning him, and he took off."

She nodded again, taking that bite of pizza finally. They watched her carefully, waiting to see if she would break down. Her mind was swirling with a million thoughts.

"Wh-what will you do when you find him?" she asked. Ghost looked up at the other men.

"What do you want us to do, Gracie?" asked Tango. It was so quiet at the table she had to look at each of the men to be sure they were still there. What did she want to do? She'd thought about it so many times. The pain in her chest was so intense she could barely breathe. The fear consumed her at moments, leaving her wondering if she would ever be normal again.

She looked up at the men, sitting straighter. Turning, she kissed Ghost, diving into his mouth, tongues dancing with the taste of pizza and soda. Finally, pulling back, she took a deep breath and looked at the table.

"I want to kill him."

CHAPTER FOURTEEN

Grace stood from the table, never looking up at the group of men. She left the club headed back toward the private living quarters. Ghost watched her and frowned. She didn't understand what that would do to her, having that weight on her shoulders. Kyle might be a piece of shit, but he was the father to her children, and no matter how awful he was, the heinous crime he committed, he was still the supplier of their DNA.

"Are you going to let her get the kill?" asked Zulu.

"Fuck if I know," he muttered, looking back at the table. "She wants it. I know she does, but she doesn't understand what that means. We all know. Shit, the nightmares, the eyes staring at you, the guilt of it even when it's justified. Taking a life is not what everyone thinks it is."

They all nodded, quietly eating their lunch. Gunner walked into the club and sat at the table with the others. He grabbed a slice of pizza and scarfed it down in two bites. He picked up the second slice and noticed the others staring in his direction.

"I lost him on the other side of town. He was speeding like nobody's business through Main Street, not a damned cop in sight." Zulu nodded.

"I tried to go the long route to see if he would be hiding at one of the B&Bs, but nothing. I did get the plate. It's stolen, no surprise. I called the sheriff to clear up some of the confusion. I told him to contact the detective in charge of Grace's family's murder. He said he wouldn't let anyone know she was here." Ghost nodded. Sheriff Webb was a friend of theirs and appreciated the work the men did on the side. He also served in the Air Force and was happy to provide support to fellow brothers.

"Okay, so we send out the twins to try and track this asshole down."

"We have another issue," said Tango. "The Warriors are demanding that we meet with them this weekend, here. They agreed to keep their numbers to ten, but Scar, their prez, is demanding financial compensation for the loss of those girls."

"I thought he said he wasn't dealing in fucking humans!" barked Ghost.

"Yea, I said the same thing. He said he meant to say that it was for losing the payout they would have made for allowing the girls to pass through their territory."

"That fucking little shit is dealing in humans, and I know it! We'll meet with them. That's fine. Close the bar down at ten. Have them here for ten-thirty along with ten of us. Tango, Gunner, Zulu, Eagle at the bar, Whiskey, Doc, Razor, Devil, Gunner, and Blade. The rest of you I want out of sight on the property. Zulu? Make sure you follow them in. I want to be assured that they're not bringing more with them and hiding them somewhere. I want Hawk guarding Grace the entire time."

The brows all raised in his direction. They had two ten-inch-thick steel doors separating their private space from the club. Even if they breached the first, Grace would be gone from the barn before the second was hit.

The outer fence was literally drilled into the center of the barn. Again – no one could get to the back of the barn through the front parking areas or the bar. They would lock the back steel door to the porch as well, ensuring that she was safe.

"I know she'll be behind the two steel doors, but still, I want her protected. If I know these assholes, they would use her as an excuse to get to us."

The men all stood, nodding at Ghost. The guys working at the garage made their way back to work on the current projects. The others made their way to their bikes, ready to hunt down Kyle Easton. Ghost made his way to his private residence, and hopefully, to the woman who stole his heart.

Stepping through the door, he looked down the long hallway and spotted Grace sitting outside on the porch. She was staring out at the forest, seated on the steps. Her arms were folded on top of her knees, and her chin was resting on her forearms.

Ghost opened the door, and Grace didn't even stir. He moved slowly toward her, not wanting to startle her if she were deep in thought. He perched himself next to her, mimicking her pose.

"Penny for your thoughts, baby girl," he said, turning toward her.

"I love you," she whispered.

"I know, baby girl. I love you too. Why does that have you looking so sad?" he asked, pouting at her. She grinned and nudged him.

"I guess... I guess I just realized I don't want anything to happen to you. What if Kyle were to hurt you or one of the other guys. I couldn't take that, Ghost." He pulled her closer, wrapping one big arm around her shoulders. The cooler fall temps blew a light breeze across his face, and he was happy as fuck she was sitting next to him sharing this moment.

"Baby girl, you know that we're all trained, military-trained. Most of us are former Special Forces... SEALs, Marines, MARSOC, Rangers, and even Delta. A lot of the guys don't have Special Forces training, but they're trained and deadly as all fuck, just the same. Honey, these men are the finest to ever grace an American military uniform. They know what they're doing." She nodded against his shoulder, and he steeled himself for what he had to tell her.

"Gracie, baby girl, on Saturday night, another MC is coming here to discuss some nasty business they were involved in. We don't expect things to get out of hand, but I need for you to be out of sight. I don't want to give them any leverage they could use against us in the future, and you, honey, are definitely leverage."

"Me? Why would I be leverage?" she asked, surprised.

"Gracie, honey, you are my whole world. You and this club. I couldn't stand it if anything happened to you, and believe me when I tell you, those assholes would know that within ten seconds of laying eyes on you that you are important to me. Please, baby girl, just let one of the guys watch you. Make it a movie night."

"Okay," she said quietly. "Ghost?"

"Hmm," he said into her hair.

"Take me upstairs and make love to me?" Before she could hear his answer, he had her thrown over his shoulder and was making his way down the hallway, and the whole way, Grace just laughed.

CHAPTER FIFTEEN

Three times, by her last count, three times this man explored her body in ways no one ever had, invaded it, and made her scream in relief and joy with the bliss of pleasure enveloping her body.

It was the middle of the afternoon, and they were lying in one another's arms, naked, sweaty, and wanting more. Ghost pulled her closer, her perfect breasts pressed against his chest, her leg wrapped over his hip. He felt the wetness of their lovemaking against his thigh and moaned, filling with desire once more. Never had a woman captured his attention in the way this woman did.

Grace smiled at him, her lips finding his once more. Her tongue dipped between his teeth as she explored his mouth, their tongues dancing around the flavors of their bodies. She gently shoved him to his back and placed her thighs on either side of his own, feeling his already hard cock rub her clit.

"Fuck, baby..." he groaned.

"What's the matter?" she smiled. "Am I too heavy?"

"Baby girl, you can't weigh more than a buck ten."

"See, that's why I love you; your optimism," she said, kissing him.

"That's why you love me?" he grinned.

"Well, that and..." she reached between them, squeezing his rock-hard cock, guiding it carefully down the wet slit begging for him again, "and this... this beautiful, gorgeous cock." She emphasized the 'k' in cock, and he moaned once again.

"You're so fucking hot, Gracie baby. It turns me the fuck on when you talk dirty like that."

"I never used to, you know, not before you. But you make me feel so comfortable, so loved, I love telling you what I want," she said, raising her hips slightly and slamming down to feel him hit her center. She rolled her eyes back and sat still for a moment as his fingers dug into her hips.

"Baby girl, don't ever be afraid to tell me what you want," he groaned against her lips. Tasting her, teasing her as she rocked back and forth against him. His balls were so heavy, so tight, he needed her.

"Anything?" she asked. He stopped just for a moment and opened his eyes to look into hers, filled with mischief.

"Anything," he growled.

"My ass... my ass has never been touched..." she said, rocking again.

"Is that so?" he sounded like a pre-teen going through a voice change. "Baby girl, we'll work our way up to it. I'm big. You know that. It will take us some time. But believe me when I say, I am one hundred fucking percent on board."

"Mmm, okay, oh, Eric... I'm going to cum again... Eric..." He slapped her ass, and she squealed, enjoying the feeling of the sting on her ass cheek. He started to move faster, drilling into her tight wet pussy, feeling her grip his cock tighter and tighter.

"I fucking love you, Grace, so fucking much," he growled.

"Eric!" she screamed his name as her body quaked with vibrations so deep within her core she thought she might shatter to pieces.

"That's it, baby, that's it," he cried, filling her once more with the hot liquid leaving his body. She fell against his chest, her hair wet with perspiration against her face. Ghost rolled with her body against his own, caging her to the bed. He feathered kisses down her face, neck, and back to her lips, taking command of her body once more.

"I'm so in love with you, Eric," she said with a tear in her eye.

"I know, baby girl, and I'm so in love with you too." He held her for a long time, their breathing finally reaching a manageable heart rate. She stood to head to the shower, but he pulled her back, bending her over in front of him.

Grace's body reacted immediately, her pussy wet and throbbing for his touch. He slid his big hands over both of her ass cheeks, one big finger lingering around her tight hole. She held her breath waiting for him. His finger slid inside her pussy, in and out.

"You're wet again, baby, for this. You want this?" She moaned in response as his wet finger slid into her hole again. She felt the pressure and gasped. "Breathe, baby girl, breathe."

Grace took in a deep breath leaning over the bed, her elbows now resting on the soft mattress as Ghost gripped one ass cheek from behind, his other resting cautiously, while his finger invaded her tight ass. The pressure was unlike anything she'd ever felt before, erotic and foreign.

"Fuck, baby girl, you're so fucking beautiful. I have to have you again, Grace," he said, standing behind her. She felt his rock-hard cock enter her wet pussy and turned to look over her shoulder, his face filled with ecstasy. He continued the invasion of her ass, his finger gently moving in and out.

"Oh! Oh, God! Eric, that feels so good, so good, baby. It's going to make me cum again!"

"Do it!" he yelled, slapping her ass cheek. "Do it for me, baby girl. I'm fucking ready to explode!" Before he could finish his sentence, she was screaming his name for the whole damn barn to hear, but he didn't give a fuck. He growled his response, driving into her, his finger still pumping in and out of her tight little puckered hole.

Ghost rested his sweat-covered cheek against her back and then pulled her to stand, her body leaning against his. Turning her, he lifted her in his arms, making his way to the shower. The hot spray covered their bodies, and a flash of a memory hit Grace from her first night. Ghost holding her beneath the water while Doc cleaned her. Her heart filled with love, she burrowed into him more.

"I don't want to be in here anymore," she whispered.

"Baby girl, just let me get you clean…"

"No, not here in the shower, in this room. I-I want to be in your room, with you, Ghost. I want to wake up next to you every day. I want to roll over in the middle of the night and feel your warmth next to me." She looked up at him, stroking his cheek, kissing his lips tenderly.

"Damn, baby girl, you know you don't have to ask me twice for that. Nothing would make me happier, fucking nothing!"

"Good," she said, smiling as he set her feet down in the shower, "now, can you please just promise me one thing?"

"I'll promise you the whole damn world, honey."

"No, nothing quite so extravagant. I just need you to promise to put the toilet seat down."

Ghost stared for just a second and then burst into laughter, loud, happy as fuck, laughter.

CHAPTER SIXTEEN

Saturday morning started with Ghost and Grace wrapped in one another's arms in *their* room. The rain was coming down in sheets of glass, and that was a bad fucking sign to Ghost. The Warriors were on their way to their territory, and rain would make things challenging if shit broke out. Although their small neck of Virginia was quiet, the Warriors territory covered parts of West Virginia where backwoods rules and ideals reigned.

He knew of Scar, knew what kind of soldier he'd been as well. Six years in the Army, and according to anyone and everyone, he'd been an insolent, cowardly soldier. His one small gift, his namesake, came from a small gash over his left cheek from a fragment that hit him during a firefight. Anyone he asked about the man said the same thing – he was a coward, a shitty fighter, and a worse man.

Ghost knew he was younger than his forty-six years, somewhere in the mid-thirties range. The Warriors were a legacy MC. Anyone who had a brother or father in the club could join. Not everyone served their country, but that didn't seem to matter to them. They were involved in gun-running, drugs, and now it seemed, human trafficking. None of which the Steel Patriots wanted a part of except to stop it.

Ghost watched as the men made preparations for the evening, securing gates and adding extra security cameras to the property. He saw Grace take on the afternoon shift at the bar, and secretly, he let out a sigh of relief. That would mean she would disappear around 9:30, and Eagle would be on after that.

He watched her working with the customers, some regulars, smiling and taking their orders quickly and efficiently. She really was good at the customer service aspect of the job. At five-thirty, she nodded at the door where Hawk stood checking IDs, beckoning for him to come to her. Ghost started to stand, but thinking better of it, allowed her to handle whatever issue by herself.

She spoke to Hawk in hushed tones, pointing to the man at the end of the bar, his head nearly buried in his beer.

"I've called a taxi for him, Hawk," she said quietly. "He doesn't want to go, but he's had enough. I'm not going to serve him anymore." Hawk nodded, smiling at Grace.

"Let's go, buddy," he said, lifting the man easily under his arm. "Your chariot awaits."

"W-way... wait... I didn't call a damn cherry-ot," he mumbled.

"Well, there's one with your name on it. Let's go." Hawk carried the man out, and Grace just sighed, watching him. The man had been mumbling about his wife leaving him, and she did feel sorry for him but wasn't about to let him kill himself or someone else driving back down the mountain road in the rain.

Thunder boomed outside, lightning streaking across the sky. The door opened once more, and Hawk stepped back in, nodding at Grace. He wiped his brow, and she noticed him let a little shiver escape his shoulders. He sat back on the corner stool at the bar, and she moved toward him with a cup of coffee.

"Are you okay, Hawk? Are you coming down with something?" she asked, reaching for his forehead. Hawk smiled down at the pretty woman.

"Nah, I'm good," he said, sneezing. "I've just been feeling off the last couple of days."

"Well, maybe let Doc look at you before anything gets worse, huh?" He nodded again at her and went back to reading the book he had in his hands. It was one of Grace's romance novels, one in which the sex scenes were particularly graphic and detailed.

"Umm, so, Hawk, you like romance novels?" she asked, smiling at him. He looked at the cover and shrugged.

"It's very informative," he said, grinning. "Tell me, beautiful Grace, the things that happen in these books, are they really things that women want to happen to them or done to them?" He blushed furiously, and she almost burst out laughing. If you'd asked her a year ago, she would have said no. Hell, even six months ago, she would have said no. But now? Now, she would have to say...

"Yes. I mean, not the violent stuff that happens sometimes, but I think most women are looking for a man to cherish her, treasure her, treat her like she's the only thing in his world that really matters." He nodded again and looked toward Ghost, who was speaking to the officers of the club.

"And, not to get personal, but is that how Ghost makes you feel?" She wiped another glass and set it on the counter, then picked up a wine glass filling it for the waitress.

"It is. I never had that before. No one has ever made me feel that way. You saw me, Hawk. I was broken to pieces, millions of them. I think I still am somewhat. Maybe not millions but certainly hundreds," she smiled in his direction. "Ghost lets me know every day that I'm the only woman in his life; the only person to make him feel..."

"Loved," he finished.

"Yea, loved and..." she started to speak when a voice behind her chimed in.

"Loved? Ghost isn't capable of love." Fucking hell, Amanda, thought Hawk. "He's capable of fucking. No kissing because he won't do that. Blow jobs? Oh, yea, he likes those sometimes, but love. Don't let yourself get delusional, honey."

Hawk started to stand but noticed that Grace squared her shoulders, staring down the young woman.

"And what's your name?" asked Grace.

"Amanda, I'm sure he's talked about me. We were hot together." Grace nodded.

"Well, Amanda, he hasn't spoken about you, and since we've been together months now, I would suspect that you were a former acquaintance. Now, I don't know what your mother taught you, but my mother taught me to be respectful of others and their relationships. I don't kiss and tell, and I absolutely don't walk into bars and try to destroy relationships just because it makes me happy."

"I don't…"

"Stop right there before you embarrass yourself further," said Grace. "You fucked him. You sucked his cock." Hawk nearly spit his coffee across the bar. He watched as Ghost rose from his table and started to walk their way. "I get it. You're pissed that he didn't choose you. What are you? Twenty-two? Twenty-three? Ghost is forty-six. Old enough to be your father. Now, if you have daddy issues, get help. If you have issues wanting to destroy other people's lives, get help. But let me make this clear to you, Amanda.

"If you ever fucking walk into this bar again and come at me because of my love for Ghost, you will regret it. I may look meek and small to you, but I promise you, I've kicked ass on better than you. You see, my father was a former police officer, and he taught me plenty as a young woman to keep me safe from men and women. Now take your rude, disrespectful, spiteful, hateful ass out of here."

She started to speak and then saw Ghost standing at the end of the bar.

"I thought I told you that you weren't welcome here any longer."

"I'm leaving," she said, backing up, "but it's not over, not by a long shot. You owe me."

"Doesn't that make you a whore if he owes you for favors?" asked Hawk, laughing at the woman as she headed to the door.

"Shut the fuck up, Hawk! You didn't seem to mind when I was sucking your dick."

"Nope, no man in his right mind refuses free dick sucking. But when you discover the complications with the giver, you let it go. Now get out."

She walked quickly out the door. Her thin sweatshirt pulled up over her head to protect from the rain. Grace simply went back to wiping glasses.

"Baby girl…"

"It's okay, Ghost. You have a past. I know that. She was just trying to get to me. Hawk and I had it handled. Everything is okay, I promise." She reached up and kissed him, then returned to fill the orders at the bar. Hawk sipped his coffee, smiling into the cup as he watched true love happen before his eyes.

Grace busied herself with the customers as Ghost, Hawk, and Zulu spoke.

"Does anybody else get a weird feeling that she showed up here today, the day the Warriors are coming in?" said Zulu.

"Yea, I get a fucking weird feeling, and now she's seen Grace and knows what she means to me. Fucking hell."

"Don't worry, Ghost, we'll make sure nothing happens to Grace." Hawk nodded at his president and then looked back toward the door of the bar.

"We might need to rethink the idea of the hang-arounds," said Zulu. Hawk raised his eyebrows and grinned at the big man. "Look, man, I like pussy like the rest of you, but most of these girls are used to MCs that give them rooms, protection, and sometimes make them old ladies. We might make one an old lady, but we don't put them up here because we're not using the club to fuck out in the open. No offense, but none of you are seeing my huge dick while I'm drilling into a chick."

"Dude! I do not want to see your dick any time, let alone when you're with a chick," said Hawk.

"You might be right," said Ghost. "Let's talk about this during our meeting. Right now, let's get ready for the fucking Warriors. Hawk? Take Grace upstairs. I'll watch the bar until Eagle comes back down."

CHAPTER SEVENTEEN

Grace laughed as they made their way down the hall toward Eagle's room, smiling up at Hawk as he told her stories of their twin adventures before the Army and after. Just as they reached his door, Doc stepped out.

"Oh shit, there you are!" he said, pointing to Hawk. "Inside now; you and your brother are quarantined for the next ten days."

"Quarantined! What the fuck for?" he squealed.

"Chicken pox," said Doc, looking at Grace.

"Don't worry, Doc. I've had chicken pox, both the girls had it, and I've been vaccinated as an adult, so I'm good. Can I do anything for them?"

"No," Eagles' voice filtered from the inside of the room. "We have to find someone to cover the bar," he said.

"There is no one," said Grace, biting her lip. "Everyone has a specific job tonight except me."

"You can't go down there, Grace. Ghost will lose his fucking shit if you're down there when the Warriors arrive," said Doc.

"Well then, he'll just have to lose his shit," she said with her hands on her hips. "You get them settled, and I'll go back down. Eagle? Hawk? Do as Doc says, and I'll check on you later to make sure you're okay. Remember, no scratching!"

Both men moaned as she pointed her tiny finger in their direction, shaking it at them like a mom would do. They both nodded, Hawk already peeling off his clothes and crawling into his bed.

"Ghost's gonna fucking kill me," whispered Doc, shaking his head.

"It's not your fault!" she cried. "Look, I'll be okay, I promise. I know I haven't done the weapons training with Ghost yet, but what about some mace or a knife? My dad was a cop, so I do know some basic hand-to-hand type stuff." Doc's stomach did a twirl thinking about giving Ghost's woman any type of weapon, but he'd rather she has something than nothing. He handed her his small buck knife, and she shoved it in her back pocket.

"Don't pull it unless you have to, and if you pull it, you need to be prepared to use it." She nodded and kissed his cheek, walking back down the hallway. At the steel door, she sucked in a deep breath and opened the door, heading to the bar.

Ghost was still standing behind the bar waiting for the Warriors when she walked up. He looked about as pissed as she'd ever seen him.

"What the fuck are you doing down here? We had an agreement!" he snarled. He didn't want to upset Grace, but she needed to understand the severity of this situation.

"Stop bellowing at me, and I'll tell you," she said quietly. "Hawk and Eagle are in quarantine; they have chicken pox."

"Are you fucking serious right now?" he said, grinding his teeth.

"Yes, I'm fucking serious. Doc is getting them settled. You don't have a choice, Ghost. I'm your bartender. Everyone else is working. You know that. I'll be okay with all of you here." She could tell her words were not bringing him any comfort at all.

"Look, I'll bring pitchers of beer to the tables instead of people coming up for individual orders. It might last longer that way. I'll only bring the first few orders. At midnight, I'll leave out the front door like any other employee. One of the guys can walk me through the gate to the back. No one will know I live here."

He eyed her suspiciously, nodding. It might work. If they thought she was just another employee, it would work.

"I fucking hate it, but alright." He reached for her hand, giving it a light squeeze as the door opened, and the fucking Warriors walked in with Scar leading his pack. "Be careful, baby girl. I love you."

The doors were shut and locked as the ten men took their seats around the table. Grace began pulling pitchers of beer and setting bottles of whiskey with glasses on trays. She tried not to look in their direction, keeping her head down as always. She was seriously grateful for the zippered hoodie she had on over her tank top tonight.

Moving around the bar, she picked up the first tray and moved toward Ghost's table, where Scar and three of his men were seated along with Zulu, Tango, and Gunner. Reaching the table, she set the drinks down and started to move when Scar slapped her ass. Ghost nearly came out from behind the table.

"Now that's some fine ass there. Could bounce a quarter off that," he grinned with nicotine-stained teeth.

"I'm not part of the menu," she said casually, trying to maneuver out of his reach. He gripped her arm and pulled hard.

"You're part of the menu if I fucking say you are," he growled. Before anyone could stop him, Ghost stood, his chair flying backwards. Grace knew this could end in all-out war. Thinking quickly, she twisted her arm, just like her father taught her, turning the other man's wrist so hard he couldn't even think. She held his thumb against his wrist, smiling down at him.

"As I said, I'm not part of the menu. I'm doing this as a favor to a friend. Now, please, don't make your host angry." She released his hand, and the men all gave a collective sigh of relief as the Warriors took their seats once more. But the damage was done. Scar's ego was bruised, and he was pissed.

"Is that how you let your club whores treat guests?" he yelled.

"You were told we don't have club whores," said Ghost. "It's like she said, she's covering for a sick bartender as a favor, that's all. You touch her or any other woman in this place without their permission again, and it will be seen as a serious affront to our club."

"Affront? What the fuck? You an Ivy League boy now, Ghost? You're nothing but a fucking EX SEAL. Whatever. Let's get down to business. You boys intercepted some cargo traveling through my territory that was earmarked for a friend. It was bought and paid for, and we guaranteed delivery. You owe us for the cargo."

"I don't owe you shit," said Ghost, gritting his teeth. He saw in his periphery that Grace was now shadowed by Doc, who followed her from table to table as she set down the beer and whiskey. It made him feel somewhat better knowing she was covered. "You were fucking trafficking those women, and we are paid to stop that shit, and we did. Now, if you'd like to go to the feds and make a claim, I'm sure they'd listen to you, but you can be assured, I will not give you a fucking dime for you dealing in young girls."

Scar was breathing heavily, rubbing the small scar on his cheek. Grace thought it was ridiculous. It was all posturing and dick-showing, but she knew enough to keep her mouth shut. This man was obviously very different from the men she'd come to know and love in the club. If he were dealing in human trafficking, he was the lowest form of life.

"Seems we are at a big disagreement, my friend…"

"I'm not your friend, and just for future reference, there is no such thing as a *former* SEAL."

"Or former MARSOC," said Whiskey.

"Or Ranger," said Doc. The heads of other members of the Warriors turned, some looking slightly impressed, others looking more afraid. Good – they should be fucking afraid.

"Yea, yea, whatever, Ghost. You're a big bad SEAL, big fucking deal. I'm talking about here and now, today. You entered my territory and took my shipment. Mine!" he yelled, slamming the table, causing the glasses to clink together. To Ghost's credit, he and his team didn't move a muscle while the other men in the room all jumped.

"I see," said Ghost, smiling, "I get it now. You were paid for those girls, and you spent the money. I'm gonna guess you spent it on drugs. Which are now gone, either used or sold. Your buyer for the women is pissed, and I'm going to guess he's not somebody you want to piss off."

"Fuck you, asshole!"

"Nasty, nasty," said Ghost. "Who is it? Who was your buyer?"

"No one you know," growled Scar.

"Oh, you'd be surprised who all I know. See, I didn't sever all my military ties when I left. I still have plenty of friends in DC who can make your fucking life miserable. DEA, Homeland. Just give me one reason, and I'll make the call."

Scar stared at the man across the table from him. He hated him… hated him with all that he could muster. But he also knew that he was speaking the truth. He had connections to the feds that Scar did not, and the truth was, he could make his life miserable.

"You need to help me out here, Ghost. I need something to make up for the lost shipment. Guns? Drugs? Something," he said, eyes wandering towards Grace.

"You get fucking nothing from me," growled Ghost. "We don't deal in any of that shit. I won't tell you again. Stop your illegal shit or know that I may be at your back door every fucking time."

Ghost watched as Scar followed the figure of Grace out the front door, Zulu following closely behind her. He smiled to himself, knowing that Scar would think he had her dead to rights.

"Fine, fine," he said, raising his hands. "Just remember, you started this." He stood and moved toward the door where Zulu was coming back inside. Zulu watched as the men left the bar and then followed outside to lock the gates. Coming back inside, he locked the door.

Ghost sent a text to Grace that it was safe to come back down, and he waited to see her beautiful face once more. She'd been so brave and handled herself perfectly with the little shit, Scar.

"What do you think, Ghost?" asked Doc.

"I think the prick is serious. He wants war over this. Get Ace to see if he can track down who his potential buyer was. If we can do that, we might be able to work it from the other side of the table." Doc nodded, rising to head to the security room.

Ghost turned to see the beautiful woman walking through the steel door. Her smile was shaky, but she seemed intent on holding her ground, and then just as suddenly, took off toward his open arms, grabbing his shoulders as tightly as she could. He swung her around, gripping her body tightly to his own.

"I was so scared I did something wrong," she cried into his neck.

"You did nothing wrong, baby, nothing. I'm so fucking proud of you," he said into her lips. They held each other for what seemed like forever. When Ghost set her feet on the floor, they turned to see that everyone was gone. The music played softly behind them, and he held her hand in his, his arm still snaked around her waist, swaying softly to the music.

Doc and Tango watched from the doorway, nudging one another.

"Beautiful fucking sight, ain't it, Doc?" said Tango.

"Something I never thought I'd see for sure, Tango. What about you, man? You want that?" he asked his friend.

"You know, I believe I do."

CHAPTER EIGHTEEN

Grace and Ghost spent all of Sunday in bed together, the rain still coming down in sheets of cold pellets. They watched movies, spoke of their childhoods, and even discussed what their future might look like together.

Three days later, as Grace made her way downstairs for breakfast, she ran into Doc as he was leaving the room for Eagle and Hawk.

"How are they?" she asked, smiling at him.

"They're little assholes is what they are," he said. "I told them both not to scratch, and what are they doing?"

"Scratching?" she replied with a grin.

"Yes! I showed the little bastards, I taped their hands up with cotton. Good luck with that shlt," he smiled. Grace grinned back and pointed to the door with a 'may I' expression. Doc nodded as she opened the door and smiled. The twins were rubbing their backs against the walls like a couple of grizzly cubs.

"You little shits! I told you that it will leave scars! Stop that!" Grace stepped inside the room, hands at her hips.

"Stop that right now!" she yelled. Eagle and Hawk both stopped, staring at the tiny woman in the middle of their room. "You heard Doc. All that scratching will lead to scarring. Do you want to be scarred for life? Women aren't crazy about scars, you know. Do as you're told, or I swear I will come up here and guard you both for the remainder of the time and force you to watch Lifetime movies."

"Grace," whispered Hawk, "that's just fucking mean. I thought you were nice."

"I am nice when you do as you are told. I'm going to leave the door open, and I'm going to tell EVERYONE in the club that you two are not supposed to scratch. If they find you scratching, that's one movie for each of you. If you, by some stupid mistake, hit ten movies, I will make you watch the entire holiday series of movies on the romance channel."

"Shit," said Eagle under his breath, "she's fucking brutal." Doc could only smile.

"Alright then, we have an understanding. Do something to occupy your mind. Read or watch movies or listen to music. But do not scratch. I'll be back when you least expect me." She walked out of the room, winking at Doc only to run straight into the chest of Ghost.

He smiled down at her, taking her hand in his to head to breakfast.

"That was pretty badass, baby girl," he said, smirking at her.

"You just have to know how to handle them," she smiled. "Those two especially are still just kids themselves."

"Gracie," said Doc, "they might look like kids, but those two served in some of the worst fights in the sandbox.

"I know what you're saying, Doc, but that doesn't mean they aren't still kids at heart. Shoot! All of you are to some degree."

"I don't know, baby; I think we're all grown-ass men." Grace said nothing but just nodded.

"I was thinking I might bake some chocolate chip cookies today since fall is here. It feels like cookie season."

"Cookies!" came the cry. "Yes, fucking cookies!"

"Can we have peanut butter cookies, Grace?" asked Zulu.

"No way, we need oatmeal raisin," said Doc. Grace stood with her arms crossed over her chest, and a collective groan was heard around the room.

"Okay, baby girl," said Ghost, grinning, "you made your point. But seriously, will you make cookies?" Grace could only laugh as she sat down with the guys for breakfast. As dishes were cleared, she smiled at George as he pulled out cookie sheets.

"Thank you, George," she laughed.

"Hey, don't think I don't want some damn cookies too! These boys don't do sweets much, mostly cuz I don't make 'em but feel free, Gracie." She loved that they all called her Gracie. It made her feel as though she had twenty big brothers, although most were younger than her.

"Hey, Grace," said Doc, coming back into the room, "I have someone that is willing to come out and conduct therapy sessions here for you, but she really wants to visit with you in her office for the first visit. Would you be willing? A few of us can go with you."

Grace swallowed hard, her heartbeat speeding up inside her chest. She felt the sweat building on her forehead and then felt the big warm hand of George on her back.

"It's okay, Gracie girl. These boys will take care of you." She smiled at the big man and nodded.

"Yes, yes, okay, I'll do the first visit in the office."

"Okay then, I'll arrange for something this week. I'm sure Ghost will go with you, but we'll probably send a few boys just to be sure all is good." Grace nodded and then decided cookies were a great idea. Baking would distract her from what was happening and what she would have to face outside the fence.

Yep, outside the fence for the first time in nearly four months.

CHAPTER NINETEEN

Kyle Easton crouched lower in the front seat of the stolen car. Fast food wrappers littered the floorboards, the smell of body odor filled the space. He couldn't remember when he'd last brushed his teeth or taken a shower. Thanks to Grace, he had no money, no job, and no way to return to his own home.

His shoulder screamed at him, the ache coming from the stab wound the little bitch gave him. With the colder weather and rain, he felt the ache even more so. Now he just watched from the vacant driveway across the road.

The business at the Steel Garage seemed brisk, and people came and went, seemingly happy with the service. He couldn't tell if they were just a bunch of motorcycle hoodlums or just grungy businesspeople, but he knew that Grace was in that building, and he was going to fucking get to her one way or another.

He thought about just walking through the front door of the bar but realized that would be too difficult. If she had only allowed him to see his children, none of this would be happening. She was always so unreasonable.

The receptionist he'd fucked in the supply closet was a complete fluke. Well, it was a fluke he got caught. He'd done it plenty of times before, but every man did. His own father had two mistresses on the side before the old man split. Grace was the woman for him, and she would see it once again.

When she got pregnant with the twins, he knew his life was fucking screwed. He wanted her pregnant with one so she would marry him, but when he found out they were having twins, he decided he'd stick around and try to make the best of it. Unfortunately, she wanted more fucking kids, and he wasn't about to let that happen, so he got himself snipped.

When she went for tests to see if there was something wrong with her, he simply intercepted the letter from her gynecologist and replaced it with a forged one stating that she could no longer have children. Easy. Gullible Grace believed him, and he was able to fuck her when he wanted or more like when she wanted. The bitch pushed him away the last few years.

He tried to be present for his daughters, tried on multiple occasions to see them and be part of their lives. But every time Grace would stop him from coming inside the house, every fucking time. Her damn father had ties to the police department, and that created more issues for him, allowing her to get the restraining order against him. He'd even tried to see the girls at school, but the school had strict instructions to not allow him near them without Grace's approval.

Who needs approval to see their own fucking children? Well, he fixed that. He made sure she was gone when he drove to see the girls on their graduation day. The little bitches were just like their mother, though, stopping him from coming inside the house. Where there's a will, there's a way.

So, he hopped the fence and killed the old man first, then shot good old grandma. His girls huddled together, holding each other's hands. They refused to go with him, so what choice did he have? He shot them. They were gone now, out of his way, and there was nothing that could keep him from Grace. It was so easy breaking into the house after the funerals, her drunk ass laid out like a buffet on the bed. He should have fucked her then.

He hadn't expected her to fight back in that little cabin of his. He'd tried several times to fuck her there, but each time she'd cry and kick out, making his dick soft. It was her fault he couldn't fuck anymore. Her fault he wasn't hard enough.

He'd never had problems pleasing women before. That was until Grace divorced him and kicked him out. Now, he had to have those damn pills to get him hard, and even then, the side effects weren't worth it for him. He tried getting hard just by looking at Grace in the cabin. He'd stripped her and rubbed his dick until it was raw. He waited for her to wake up and suck his dick, but he'd hit her so hard she wouldn't come around.

Then the whore definitely got the jump on him with the knife. The aching scar on his shoulder was evidence of that. Now, he just needed to find a way into that bar, so he could get his wife and get out of this little town.

Yes, sir, Grace would be Mrs. Kyle Easton once more.

CHAPTER TWENTY

Grace had never ridden on the back of a motorcycle before, and it was exhilarating. It was also freaking cold! She wore a warm fleece-lined coat with a scarf and gloves, as well as the helmet, and she was still freezing! She wrapped her arms around Ghost and held on for dear life. As the vibration of the motor lulled her into comfort, she became more at ease as the ride went on, she relaxed and enjoyed it more and more. Always in front was Gunner and to the rear of their bike were Doc and Zulu.

Grace saw, for the first time in the light of day, their little mountain community. There was a quaint Main Street with small cafes and boutiques, a tiny flower shop, a bakery, and even a salon. She didn't remember much about the mall trip with Doc having her hide herself in the back of his SUV, but she would remember this.

She could see that that town was preparing for fall festivals, and that made her heart sing. This was the type of community she's always wanted to live in. As they passed people on Main Street, hands raised in a friendly wave, and Grace felt what she already knew; the community respected these men.

The bikes pulled into the medical building parking lot and found spots as close to the door as was available. Ghost held out his hand to help Grace off the back of the bike and then took her helmet, securing it inside the locked container.

"That was amazing!" she said, smiling at them. "That was so much fun! I can't wait until we can go for a long ride in the summer."

"I'm glad you liked it, Gracie girl," said Gunner. "I'll stay down here with the bikes while you guys go up." He nodded at Ghost, and Grace wondered why he would need to stay with the bikes. Too nervous to think of anything other than her visit, she simply followed Doc, Ghost holding her hand.

"So, Grace, this doctor has been a therapist for about ten years now. She specializes in women who have endured traumatic events. I don't know her personally, but an old buddy of mine from the Army said she was top notch."

"I trust you, Doc," she said, biting her lip. "I'm just really nervous."

"I know you are, Gracie girl, but she just needs to get this big visit done, and then she'll come out and see you. I think it has something to do with hospital policy since she's affiliated with Mountain General." Grace nodded again, and as the elevator doors opened, they stepped down the hallway to a small office.

The waiting area only had four seats, so it was good that Gunner had stayed downstairs. She pressed the button by the door as indicated and watched it light up. Taking her seat, she gripped Ghost's fingers as if she were falling down a black hole.

"It's okay, baby girl. I'm here." He kissed her forehead, and she smiled, nodding again.

The door opened, and a tall curvy redhead stood smiling at them. She wore a simple navy-blue dress with a white blouse beneath, the collar popped at her neck. Her long, curvy legs were bare, her feet tucked into a pair of professional yet sexy as fuck navy heels. Her fire engine hair fell to the middle of her back, her hazel eyes staring at the room of people. Her bright smile went from face to face, stopping briefly at Doc's handsome face. She nodded at the room.

"Well, I have to assume that you're Grace," she said with an outstretched hand. "I'm Dr. Aubrey Collins, but my friends just call me Bree."

"Hi, Bree, yes, I'm Grace, and these are my friends and this is my…"

"Fiancé," said Ghost. He smiled at Grace, and she blushed furiously.

"Well, it's very nice to meet you. Will you all be staying while we're in session?" she asked.

"If it's okay with you, doc, we'd like to," said Doc. "I'm Doc, by the way. Uh, I mean, Jack Harris. I think our mutual friend Dr. Yost reached out to you."

"Yes, yes, he did! I'm so glad we were able to connect, and it's no problem at all for all of you to stay. In fact, I might ask you…"

"Ghost."

"Ghost? Okay, Ghost, we might ask you to step in toward the end of the session. We'll see how things go." She moved into the space behind her and closed the door as the three men looked at one another.

Concern filled the face of Ghost, wondering if Grace would be okay with the doctor alone. Appreciation filled the face of Zulu at the gorgeous assets displayed by the beautiful doctor. But it was lust that filled the face of Doc, pure unadulterated lust.

"Holy shit, she's fucking hot," muttered Zulu.

"Yea, she's… she's shit…" Doc couldn't find his words, and Ghost looked at his friend and grinned. Oh, this would be good if Doc actually fell. Although he was two years older than Doc, Ghost was always close with the man and felt they were like blood brothers.

Zulu looked down at his phone and muttered a curse under his breath.

"Tango thinks he saw Kyle in a car parked across the street watching the property. He started to walk over to ask what he was doing, and he took off. I think he knows Grace is with us."

Ghost said nothing, standing to pace the small box of a waiting room. He knew that Grace wanted to kill Kyle, but he just couldn't let her do it. She would have to live with that for the rest of her life.

"Let him sit there if he comes back. We're going to take care of him ourselves. Tell Tango to watch for him, have Ace watch the security videos, pan out further. If we see him, just let him sit there. We're going to end him, not Grace. I'm not going to put that burden on her."

Zulu nodded sending the text to Tango.

CHAPTER TWENTY-ONE

"So, Grace, why don't we start with you just telling me what brings you here? Whenever you're ready, you just tell me what you want me to hear. Okay?" Grace nodded at the pretty doctor and realized that she was probably a good five or six years younger than her own forty-one years. She certainly was beautiful.

"I... I guess I start from the beginning, right?" Grace smiled at the woman as she nodded. "I was married once a long time ago. We dated while I was in college, and Kyle pushed for me to get married, but I really didn't want to."

"Why was that?" she asked.

"I don't know. Thinking back, I guess I just didn't feel like he was the 'one.' Anyway, I got pregnant and found out later that he tampered with my birth control to force me to accept marriage. I guess I still didn't need to say yes, but it seemed the right thing to do. It was the second trimester before I discovered I was pregnant with twins."

"Wow, that must have been a wonderful surprise!"

"It..." Grace wiped a tear and continued. "Kyle had trouble keeping a job. It was always something. He was drinking on the job or would get caught with marijuana. The last incident, he was fired because he got caught in the supply closet with the receptionist."

"Ouch. How did that make you feel, Grace?"

"Hurt, used, sick, angry... I think just disappointed with myself more than anything. I suspected what he was and what he was doing, but I just never faced up to it. This sort of forced me to do that. I filed for divorce and full custody of the girls, which I got because he had no way to support them. He would come in and out of their lives sporadically, but he was violent with me, always trying to hit me when he was around me. It was as if I made a switch go off in him, and he'd be violent."

"You were the one that got away, Grace. He wasn't angry as much with you as he was with himself for letting you leave. Doesn't excuse his behavior, but it wasn't you." She nodded and continued.

"In June of this year... my girls... Faith and Hope, they were graduating from high school and heading to college. First, though, they were going to travel around Europe. It was a trip we'd planned for months."

"That's exciting! I remember doing the same thing," she said, smiling enthusiastically at the other woman.

"Yes, well, Kyle called and wanted to come to their graduation party. The girls specifically asked that I not invite him. They didn't want the drama. I left the house to pick up the cake, and he called. He was so angry with me, so mad that I wouldn't let him come to the party. He said, 'this is your fault.

"I just knew something was wrong. I raced home from the bakery, and police vehicles were swarming my house. My neighbor heard the commotion and called 911 and then went over to my house. Kyle... he shot both my parents, my neighbor, and... both the girls." Grace wiped the tears threatening to spill.

"Oh, Grace," said Aubrey, reaching for her hand, "I'm so sorry for your loss, honey. That must have been horrible."

"It wasn't the end. The night after the funerals, I came home and locked myself inside the house. I grabbed a bottle of whiskey and just drank and drank. I don't even remember how it happened, but somewhere in the night, Kyle broke in and took me. He held me captive for ten days, beating me, cutting me, and trying to rape me. He didn't succeed, but every time he failed, he'd beat me again."

Aubrey swallowed hard, watching Grace tell the story stoically and bravely. It had been several months, so she was holding it together fairly well, but in Bree's experience, she would break down again sooner or later.

"I had a window of opportunity to escape, and I took it, stabbing him. I drove and drove. Hours, days until I crashed the car from exhaustion. Then I just walked. There was this light on a hill... an old garage. Behind it was a barn, but it was surrounded by this security gate. I remember walking up to it, and this sweet young man just picked me up and took me inside.

"Those men... the ones in the waiting area... they nursed me back to health, kept me safe. Ghost is more than I could have ever prayed for, and believe me, I prayed for a lot in those first few weeks. He was so kind and sweet and tender with me. We fell in love. We are in love."

"What a beautiful gift to come from something so horrendous, Grace."

"He's still out there... Kyle. He's still trying to get to me, and they're still protecting me. It's why Doc asked you to come to the barn." Bree looked at her, confused. "The barn is on their property. It's huge. There's a bar at the front, Club Steel, and then there are residences at the back and upstairs."

"I see," said Bree, nodding. "And you feel safe in this place?"

"I do. I've never felt safer."

"Then what do you want to come from all this, Grace? What's your ultimate goal? It doesn't have to be one goal, it can be several. Do you want to be able to have intimacy with Ghost?"

"Oh," she said, blushing, "actually, we're okay in that department. He's the most incredible man I've ever been around, and I was comfortable with him right away. He didn't touch me in a sexual way for almost two months. Even then, he let me make the first move.

"No, no, I need help just regaining my independence. I don't want to be afraid every time a man walks by me. I want to be able to go into a store and not be terrified that I won't make it out again. I... I want to remember my daughters and my parents, but I don't want to drown in those memories."

Bree nodded again and wrote swiftly on the pad balanced on her knee.

"You seem to be doing remarkably well, Grace. I see a lot of patients who aren't where you are years after an incident. I think what Ghost and the others have done for you has provided exactly what you needed. Safety and comfort while you heal at your own pace. The rest of the things, we can work towards those with exercises. Is Kyle in police custody?"

"No," said Grace, taking in a deep breath, "in fact, that's part of the problem. He's still out there, and he's searching for me. We know that already. I think knowing he was captured would help me, but he just seems to be able to avoid capture." Bree nodded once more, continuing to write.

"Well, I think you're well on the road to healing, Grace. You've made remarkable progress on your own. You should be very proud of yourself. How do you feel about bringing Ghost in for a few minutes?" Grace nodded as Bree stood and opened the door, calling Ghost in.

"Hi, baby girl," he said, kissing her sweetly. "All okay?" She nodded, smiling at Bree.

"Ghost, do you have another name?" asked Bree.

"Yes, sorry, Eric."

"Eric. Okay, Eric, you've done a remarkable job with Grace, helping her to heal and making her feel safe. I think she's done an amazing job of taking care of herself as well. I want to approach her healing from two perspectives. The first is getting her to feel more confident in her safety and independence."

Ghost started to speak, but Bree held up a hand.

"I know that her ex-husband is still out there. I'm not suggesting anything right now. However, I might suggest things like the two of you going to dinner once a week or for ice cream. Simple, easy getaways without the entourage," she said, smiling at the door.

"Okay, okay, we can do that. What's the other thing?"

"I want to make sure that Grace understands that nothing, not one thing that happened, was her fault. Nothing, Grace, not one thing." Grace smiled at Bree and nodded, tears filling her eyes.

"Thank you, Bree," she said, gripping the hand of the other woman. "When can we speak again?"

"Well, since I'll come to you for the foreseeable future, how about every Wednesday at three p.m.? I can stop by Club Steel on my way home and see you, then maybe enjoy one of your famous burgers." Ghost laughed, and Grace smiled at the other woman.

"That sounds perfect," said Grace, rising to shake her hand. "Thank you, Bree. Truly, thank you. I've told my story, but for some reason, it was different telling it to you."

"I'm happy I could help, Grace, and I look forward to seeing you all next week." She opened the door to see the two leather-clad, muscle-bound men standing and staring directly at her. "Hello, gentlemen, I hope you weren't too bored."

"Nope," said Doc, smiling.

"Alright then, I'll see you next week, Grace, and maybe I'll see the rest of you as well."

Doc smiled at the woman, nodding his head. Damn straight, she'd see him next week. Even if he had to tie everyone else down by the gate, he would see this woman again.

CHAPTER TWENTY-TWO

Ghost watched as Grace made her way toward the kitchen. She seemed in good spirits after the first session with Bree, but he knew that the emotions would flood her eventually. Losing your children in the way she had was more than most would be able to survive. Top that with losing your parents as well, and she was headed for a crash.

He turned to look at the table of men he called brothers. The club was closed until two, so they had the whole place to themselves.

"Where are we at with Kyle?" he asked.

"It's like the guy is getting help from someone," said Razor. "He was staying at some run-down motel outside of town for two nights and then left a week ago. From there, he went to a little place three towns over, stayed two nights, and left again. He uses a stolen credit card every time, which means sooner or later, he'll be caught by the police if he's not caught by us."

Ghost nodded his head thinking about the information Razor was giving him. If he was only staying two nights in each location, they might be able to predict where he would be next and set a trap.

"What are you thinking?" asked Gunner.

"It's not like we live in a major city. There are probably fifty motels in a thirty-mile radius. We can eliminate the ones he's already stayed at, but if we pass around his photo to the others, we might get a hit when he checks in."

"It's a thought, although we might be putting the motel operators in danger if he notices them acting suspiciously," said Tango.

"It's worth a try. Blade? You've been itching for a long ride," he said, staring at the other man.

"On it." Before he could even wish him good luck, Blade was gone.

"Where are we at with the Warriors?" asked Ghost.

"My contact says the whole fucking club is ready to implode. Probably eighty percent of the guys hate Scar but are too afraid to go up against him. They actually want him gone. He's talking about bringing down the entire club on us," said Tango.

"Ace? Any idea who his buyer for the girls is?"

"Yep," he said with a satisfied smile. "Anton Krevnyv."

"Fuuuuccckkkk! Please, tell me you're joking," said Ghost, standing, running his fingers through his hair.

"Wish I was. Krevnyv paid a hundred thousand for the girls, and it appears Scar immediately spent that hundred grand on heroin, most of which he sold, some of which he used himself. Krevnyv is watched by Homeland and the FBI. Our guy there says that he's furious that Scar took his money but didn't deliver the merchandise."

"Is he reasonable?" asked Ghost. Eyebrows raised around the room, and chairs shifted against the wood floor. "I mean, reasonable enough to speak with us?"

"I'm not sure," said Ace. "I can contact our friends in DC and get some intel on him. He's got his hands in everything. He has no reason to be pissed with us. We did our jobs, but he might not see it that way."

"See what we can find on him – everything. I want to know about his family, his bank accounts, who he sells to, what he sells, everything."

"We're treading into dangerous waters, Ghost," said Gunner. "This guy is global. He's not some small-time criminal in backwoods, West Virginia. He's big and has far-reaching arms. Do we really want to open this Pandora's box?"

"I know, but it's either this, or we go to war with the Warriors. Now, we all know that we're more than capable of taking them out, but I won't risk losing some of our own men to do that." Ghost walked around the group one more time, pacing like a caged lion. "If we can get Krevnyv to listen to us, just hear us out, we might be able to turn this whole situation around at the Warriors."

"I might have something," said Whiskey as he slid his phone in his back pocket. "A guy we met in the sandbox, Ivan Pechkin, he was working with the Brits but was born in Russia. I sent a message to him asking if he knew anything about Krevnyv. He suggested we speak in person. He's in DC now. I can get there by tomorrow and be back here by the weekend, hopefully with some news."

"Okay. Whiskey? Take Ace with you. We have no clue what those assholes, the Warriors, might do. Watch your six and call in every four hours. I want to know where you're staying and that you're safe." Both men nodded and headed toward their rooms to pack. "We're going to hold off on doing anything until we get the information back from Whiskey and Ace. Until then, business as usual."

The men scattered back to work; some now off duty moved toward their rooms. Tango stood next to Ghost, watching as the guys moved away.

"What do you think?" he asked.

"I think the fucking Warriors are in over their heads, and the assholes don't even know it. I think Krevnyv knew it going in and was going to work it in his favor. If it turns out that was his intention, to fuck with them, well then, it's not our problem. I will, however, have to let him know that if we encounter another shipment of women, we will intercept, and I'm sure that's going to piss home off big time."

"Well, we never liked doing things the easy way," smiled Tango.

"Fucking truth."

CHAPTER TWENTY-THREE

Grace busied herself around the room, straightening the small apartment that she now shared with Ghost, fixing the pillows she'd ordered online, which he teased her about. Looking around the cramped space, she smiled, feeling as though it were looking more and more like home, but reality struck that her home was still waiting for her back in Alabama.

According to Detective Sanders, it was locked up tight, just waiting for her to return and pack things up. Ghost was paying for the utilities to keep it safe as well as the insurance, but sooner or later, she needed to make some decisions.

The problem was she didn't want to go back and pack things up. She didn't want to see the memories, the blood. None of it. In her heart, she knew that there were some good things in the house that she wanted to remember, but there were also memories that would cripple her if she had to face them again.

In her mind, she walked through the home that she once shared with her daughters. She would open the front door they painted together, bright yellow insets trimmed in white, inviting, welcoming. They would move into the open area of the living, dining and kitchen areas. While she made dinner, the girls would tell her about their day and talk about their upcoming adventure in Europe, their new crushes, who was dating whom, which one of them would get a boyfriend first.

She would make her way down the long hallway, lined with photographs – eighteen years of memories in black and white, and color. Each of the girls had their own rooms, Faith's always neat as a pin, Hope's a virtual petri dish of mess.

The memories... all the memories...

Grace felt the emotions bubbling to the surface and tried to push them back down, tried not to drown in them, but she couldn't control it. The tears started to fall and then the loud sobs, painful, gut-wrenching sobs. No matter how hard she tried, she couldn't stop it. The need to scream, the need to yell as if expelling the demonic memories filling her head. She heard a distant sound but couldn't pull herself free.

"Gracie, Gracie, honey," said Hawk, Eagle at his side. They were colored pink by the calamine lotion covering their bodies, but she barely noticed.

"Oh, Grace," said Eagle, holding her to his chest.

Doc came running, chasing the twins down the hall, thinking they were trying to escape. He stood in the doorway and waited. Grace let out another cry of pain and anguish, and he couldn't take it anymore. He'd watched men lose limbs in the middle of fucking nowhere, insignificant country, soldiers bury their brothers on foreign soil, or at least what was left of them; he'd heard the wailing cries of widows, but this was more than he could bear.

Doc sat on the other side of Grace and pulled her into his arms.

"Gracie, baby, what brought this on?" he asked. She shook her head, crying harder, her body shuddering against his own.

"I-I don't know. I was thinking of the girls. My pictures in my house back home, my memories. Oh God! Doc, when will I be able to have memories without them torturing me, killing me?"

"I don't know, honey, it's a good question to talk to Bree about. What I do know is that you're okay. What you're experiencing is normal, and you need to know that the way you're reacting is okay. We're okay with it, Gracie."

"Okay? I'm so far from okay, Doc. Poor Ghost... p-poor Ghost has to put up with this... th-this mess of a woman... th-this pathetic..."

"Beautiful, smart, fucking awesome woman. That's what I *get* to put up with. And you have to put up with my alpha male, cussing, fighting mess of a man." Ghost smiled at his friends, holding, comforting his woman; he didn't move, didn't try to make them move. He just watched as they helped Grace through this moment.

"Oh G-Ghost... I'm s-so sorry... I fell... fell ap-part..."

"Baby girl, I know. We all fall apart, every one of us now and then. We're here to help you pick up the pieces. If you want the things in your home, baby girl, we'll send a few guys to pack it all up and drive it back. If you don't want it, we'll just box it up and put it in storage. If you want it burned to the ground, we'll burn it to the ground. Simple as that."

She looked at Eagle, Hawk, and Doc, wiping her nose on her sleeve; she smiled, and then kissed each man's cheek, standing, she moved toward Ghost as he opened his arms and held her to his chest.

"How did I ever find you? Of all the places I might have landed, how did I get put here in your arms?"

"I don't know, baby girl, but happy as fuck you did land here." Ghost continued to hold her as his friends made their way out of the room. "What do you say we do that dinner date tonight? We can change our clothes and head into town to Angelo's. It's a little Italian place with great food and a quiet atmosphere." She leaned back and smiled up at him.

"I think that sounds amazing. Are you sure it's okay?"

"It's fine, baby girl, trust me."

"Okay, I'm going to take a nap. All this crying is exhausting," she said, smiling at him through the red nose and eyes. "I'll be ready for six. Is that okay?" He kissed her as she burrowed down into their covers.

"Perfect, Gracie girl." He closed the door to their apartment and saw Hawk, Eagle, and Doc standing to the side of the door. "Thanks for being there for her."

"Don't be an asshole," said Eagle. "She's our girl too, not like you, but you know. We heard her cries, and I gotta tell you, it's not something I ever want to hear coming from her again." Ghost nodded as the twins headed back to their room.

"She'll be okay, Ghost. I think her session with Bree probably brought up a lot of emotion. It may happen the first few times. You should be prepared for that, but just know that she needs the emotional release. It's good for her." Ghost nodded again as Doc moved down the hallway.

He was going to make it right for this woman. He didn't know how, but he would figure it out even if it took a lifetime.

CHAPTER TWENTY-FOUR

Isaac "Scar" Carter paced back and forth in his room nervously. The last hit was wearing off, his arm on fire and itching like a motherfucker. Those bastards, the Steel Patriots, were going to pay for stealing the merchandise. It was his club's way to the big time. A man like Krevnyv could make or break their club. If Scar had his way, he would make them.

Scar had visions for their futures. He wanted to be known as the premier one-percenter club on the East Coast. Badass, former military, most of them anyway, turned mercenaries, guns for hire, willing to do any job and no problem killing for it.

The problem was the do-gooder Steel Patriots and the fucking asshole Ghost. Special Forces guys were always a little condescending toward the rest of the military, but Scar felt like Ghost and his crew were even more so. They made a name for themselves as the Good Samaritan club, as well as a garage that built some of the finest bikes in the country.

If you wanted something in this world, you had to take it. That's what Scar did. He took whatever he wanted. He returned from the military and joined the Warriors working his way up the line until he was his own father's second-in-command. The old man had narrow visions, though, and Scar knew the club needed to be taken to the next level.

When the old man refused to hear his ideas for running drugs and women, he simply disposed of him in the old-fashioned, biblical sense. No one even suspected anything. I mean, the man smoked three packs a day and drank like a dying man. Which, in hindsight, was true. A few drops of the drugs he wanted to sell, and it was done.

He continued to pace, his body starting to need the fix more and more frequently. If he couldn't get more, he'd have to resort to stealing. He knew when Krevnyv's next shipment was coming through because his men were escorting it. Five hundred pounds of pure heroin with a nice barrel full of oxy and a few boxes of some other mixed assortments.

His mind wandered from one thought to the next – the Patriots, Krevnyv, his own men, the little whore who embarrassed him at the Patriot's club, the drugs, always back to the drugs. He needed the whore. He needed that tight ass beneath him, screaming for him.

Maybe he could pretend there was an intercept on the drugs and blame it on the Patriots. Yea, yea, that just might work. He could take the transport himself, just him and two of his most trusted, Hammer and Digger. Yea, that would work. Right now, though, he needed another fix himself. He heard the faint knock at the door.

"What?" he yelled.

"Scar, it's me, Amanda. I got your stuff, baby," said the meek little voice. He gripped the door handle and flung it open, grabbing her by the throat and pulling her inside.

"Give it to me!" he yelled. She handed the bag to him, her hands shaking almost violently. She started to turn and leave when he gripped her wrist, squeezing, pulling her back into his body.

"Ow! Scar, baby, you're hurting me," she whimpered.

"You think I give a fuck about that?" he asked. "Get it ready, now! Tell me about the girl, the one in the bar."

"I-I don't know anything other than her name. Grace, that's all I know, and I know that Ghost loves her."

"Fuck that shit! She'll be my sweet piece of ass soon. Fix my shit!"

She nodded, heating the spoon to melt the small crystal rock. Scar tied the rubber tube around his own arm, slapping the crease of his elbow, the big vein popping to attention like a good little soldier.

Amanda drew up the liquid and started to hand it to Scar, but not before he pulled her onto the bed with him. He tied another rubber piece around her arm, and she squirmed.

"Please, p-please, Scar, don't do this. I don't wanna do this. I don't mind a little weed, but not this," she pleaded.

"Shut the fuck up! You're gonna get high with me, and I'm gonna show you a real good time, baby," he growled. Sticking the needle in her arm, he fed her only a little, wanting the rest for himself. Her eyes rolled back in her head, and he smiled as he let the needle continue its own magic on his body. The feeling of warmth flooded his body, everything humming.

Turning to the woman next to him, he ripped the tiny scrap of material from her chest and gripped one breast forcefully, biting into the flesh as she mumbled something incoherently, or at least incoherently to him. He shoved her skirt down and ripped the panties from her body.

He wasn't even fully hard when he shoved himself into her body, pumping furiously, trying to get it harder. She moaned beneath him, and he punched her in the face, hitting her nose, on contact blood spewed all over his bed.

"Shut the fuck up! I own you. I own everyone here!" he screamed in her face. He heard the gurgling sounds of blood and her attempts to speak, to breathe, but he ignored her. Slamming into her over and over again, he flipped her body and forced himself into her tight little puckered hole. His cock was covered in blood, and it excited him.

Leaning over her body, he gripped her hair and shoved her face further into his pillow. Her weak attempts to fight were met with his psychotic laughter as he finally spilled inside her body. He laughed and laughed until he finally succumbed to the mesmerizing joy of the drug.

When he woke later, he was covered in blood, and the little whore next to him wasn't breathing. Stumbling to his bathroom, he washed his face first, then changed his shirt. Opening the door of his room, he screamed!

"Probie! Where the fuck are you?" A young man came running down the hall, his face still full of acne he was so young. "Get rid of the bitch for me." Scar walked out of the room, and the boy stood staring at the body. As Axe came toward him, he saw the fear in the boy's eyes, his pale skin glowing in the darkness of the hall.

"Holy fuck! What has he done?" asked Axe.

"I don't know, sir… he… oh God! What am I supposed to do with her?" the boy turned and doubled over, dry heaves wracking his body.

"Go get Ice… don't tell anyone else, just Ice, you hear me, boy?" The boy nodded, running toward the clubhouse. A few minutes later, Ice came down the hallway and stopped cold seeing his friend's face.

"He's out of fucking control, brother," said Axe.

"Shit!" he checked the girl for a pulse, just by some sheer chance she was alive. He shook his head at his friend and covered the girl with the sheet on the bed. "I'll get two of the boys to bury her. Fucker's gotta go, Axe." Axe nodded.

"I'll make the call."

CHAPTER TWENTY-FIVE

Ghost waited downstairs while Grace finished getting ready for their date. He'd promised the doctor that he would do the date without an entourage, but with everything happening, he just couldn't risk it. Already waiting for them near the restaurant were Doc and Zulu.

"We're going straight from here to the restaurant and back," he told Tango. "Doc and Zulu will let you know if anything happens but..." He looked over the shoulder of his friend and scowled.

"What the fuck are those two doing here?" asked Tango.

"I don't know, but let's find out. Gunner," he said, nodding to his friend. Gunner met the two men at the door, frisking them for weapons as they held up their hands. Ghost walked toward them, hands fisted at his sides.

"Ice Axe, where's your fearless leader," he smirked.

"That's what we're here to talk about, Ghost. Listen, I asked Tango not to give you my name, but I've been feeding him information for weeks now. Ice knew I was doing it. Scar is out of control, and if I didn't think someone would put a bullet in my head, I'd fucking kill him myself."

"I get it, Axe, really, but what does this have to do with us," asked Ghost.

"He killed a girl today, Ghost. A girl that used to be here, Amanda. He's hooked on his own shit, heroine mostly, but honestly, I think he's taking everything. The girl... fuck, the girl, he drugged her, raped her and then beat her."

"I'm gonna guess he doesn't know you're here," said Tango. They both shook their heads.

"No, he thinks we went to give some money to her family, tell them she got hit by a car or some shit. Poor kid didn't have any family, but he didn't know that. We told him it would keep the cops off our backs. We have two days, told him her family was in the Philly area. Fucker didn't have a clue about someone in his own clubhouse."

"So, what do you want from me?" asked Ghost.

"We need to kill him and then disband the Warriors. They're done, Ghost. Half the members are just hanging out drinking. No one is making any money, and if they are, they're stealing it from everyone else. I signed up for this to run guns, a way to make money, but when the little asshole killed his old man and then started with drugs and girls, I wanted out."

"So, why didn't you get out?" asked Gunner.

"Man, you guys don't get it. This club thinks they're a one-percenter club. The only way out is death. Now, I've made my bed. I'll find a way out if I have to, but I will not fucking deal in drugs or women any longer. I refuse," said Ice.

"And if you were given a chance at something new, something clean, would you take it?" asked Ghost with a quirk of his brow. The two men looked at one another and nodded.

"You sayin' we could come here? Be part of the Steel Patriots?" asked Axe.

"We'd have to vote on it, but if you help us end this shit, yea, I'll speak up for you at the table. We all have to work either in the bar or the garage, and you'd be asked to *stop* shipments of drugs, guns, and girls. We're legit, nothing illegal, or you're out. No drugs at all. If you're willing, I'd owe you on this one."

"I'd fucking do it in a heartbeat, Ghost," said Ice.

"Are there others?" he asked.

"None you'd want," said Axe. "Listen, most of his guys are old as fuck. I mean, over sixty, and they just hang around hoping some young thing will actually get their dick hard. There are about twenty guys in their twenties and thirties. Only half of those actually have service time, and they were all fuckups. Now don't get me wrong. I'm not spec ops like you guys, but I served eight years in the Army and did my fucking time, and I did it well." Ghost looked at Ice.

"Six years in the Navy," he said. "Honorable discharge."

"Okay then," said Ghost, staring at his beautiful woman walking towards him. She smiled and stopped at the bar, realizing he was probably talking business. God how he loved that woman. "Get with Tango and give him all the information you have. We've got someone that hopefully will get us a meet with Krevnyv. We want him to understand what's happening with Scar."

The two men nodded and then looked at Grace.

"You need to know that Scar wants her," said Ice. "He thinks she embarrassed him when we were here and has been talking about taking her for a week now. Personally, I don't think he has the mental capacity for something like that right now, but we all know what the drugs will do to you."

"Nothing will happen to that woman, brother, I promise." Axe nodded, reaching for the big man's hand and shaking.

"Thanks for believing us, Ghost, and for giving us a second opportunity."

"Don't thank me yet," he smiled. "Your initiation is you have to kiss Gunner."

"Fuck you!" said the big man, grinning. Ghost nodded at the men and headed to the bar to grab his beautiful girl. Without even having to ask, Tango sent a message to let Doc and Zulu know what was keeping them.

"Hi," she said, smiling at him. She looked well-rested and had just a dab of makeup on her fresh face. She was dressed in a dark green sweaterdress, tights, and tall riding boots. Her hair was curled around her shoulders, and Ghost thought she looked like the most beautiful creature he'd ever laid eyes on.

"You look stunning, baby girl," he whispered against her lips.

"You're pretty handsome yourself, big boy. You sure you want to go out?" she asked.

"Baby, I promised you a date night, and we're going to have a date night. Come on, I'm hungry, and I want to get you back here to ravish your body."

"None you'd want," said Axe. "Listen, most of his guys are old as fuck. I mean, over sixty, and they just hang around hoping some young thing will actually get their dick hard. There are about twenty guys in their twenties and thirties. Only half of those actually have service time, and they were all fuckups. Now don't get me wrong. I'm not spec ops like you guys, but I served eight years in the Army and did my fucking time, and I did it well." Ghost looked at Ice.

"Six years in the Navy," he said. "Honorable discharge."

"Okay then," said Ghost, staring at his beautiful woman walking towards him. She smiled and stopped at the bar, realizing he was probably talking business. God how he loved that woman. "Get with Tango and give him all the information you have. We've got someone that hopefully will get us a meet with Krevnyv. We want him to understand what's happening with Scar."

The two men nodded and then looked at Grace.

"You need to know that Scar wants her," said Ice. "He thinks she embarrassed him when we were here and has been talking about taking her for a week now. Personally, I don't think he has the mental capacity for something like that right now, but we all know what the drugs will do to you."

"Nothing will happen to that woman, brother, I promise." Axe nodded, reaching for the big man's hand and shaking.

"Thanks for believing us, Ghost, and for giving us a second opportunity."

"Don't thank me yet," he smiled. "Your initiation is you have to kiss Gunner."

"Fuck you!" said the big man, grinning. Ghost nodded at the men and headed to the bar to grab his beautiful girl. Without even having to ask, Tango sent a message to let Doc and Zulu know what was keeping them.

"Hi," she said, smiling at him. She looked well-rested and had just a dab of makeup on her fresh face. She was dressed in a dark green sweaterdress, tights, and tall riding boots. Her hair was curled around her shoulders, and Ghost thought she looked like the most beautiful creature he'd ever laid eyes on.

"You look stunning, baby girl," he whispered against her lips.

"You're pretty handsome yourself, big boy. You sure you want to go out?" she asked.

"Baby, I promised you a date night, and we're going to have a date night. Come on, I'm hungry, and I want to get you back here to ravish your body."

CHAPTER TWENTY-SIX

Grace twirled the spaghetti onto her fork and brought the noodles and sauce to her lips, moaning with satisfaction at the mix of spices and flavors.

"Baby girl, you keep moaning like that, and you and I are going to go into that bathroom and take care of some things." Ghost reached over and slid his hand up her thigh, feeling the heat coming from her apex.

"Oh, you mean this moan… mmmmhhmm sooo good," she said seductively.

"Gracie girl, you're playing with fire." He smiled at her and was happy she was feeling good enough to joke with him. If he were being honest, he was worried about her after seeing her this afternoon. Her emotions were so raw and totally on the surface he thought he might have to give her a sedative.

"Thank you for bringing me out, Ghost. This is the first real date I've had in, well, in more than ten years. And the best part is, it's a date with the man I love."

"Baby girl, you know all the right things to say, don't you? I love you too, Gracie. You're my girl, mine, and nothing will ever change that." She smiled at him, taking another bite, and then set her fork down.

"Those men you were talking to tonight, they were here the night the Warriors were here. I remember them." Ghost nodded and took another bite of his veal. "Is there something going on?"

"Gracie girl, sometimes there will be things happening in the club that I won't be able to tell you. I promise, if I can, I will. All you need to know is that those men want what we want. Hopefully, we can figure out a way to end this fucking mess before Scar does something completely stupid."

Grace simply nodded again and sipped her wine. The liquid hit her stomach, and for some reason, she didn't like the taste, pushing it aside. She'd always liked wine. One or two glasses after a hard day was always a great way to relax and sleep. For whatever reason, lately, wine wasn't her cup of tea, so to speak.

"How is everything, Ghost?" asked Angelo.

"Delicious as always, Angelo. I'd like you to meet my girl, my fiancée, Grace."

"Fiancée! This is a celebration dinner! Let me get Lidia to bring you some tiramisu for dessert. On the house." He scurried to the back of the restaurant, and Grace eyed Ghost from across the table.

"What?" he said, staring at her. "What did I do?"

"What did you do? Ghost, that's the second time you've called me your fiancée. Two times now. Two times, and yet you've never proposed to me. We've talked long-term as far as our relationship goes, but we haven't talked marriage, not once. Don't you think that's something we should have discussed? I mean, have you ever even been married?"

"Nope," he said, smiling at her. "Never been, baby girl, never wanted to be. Not until the day the good Lord placed this green-eyed beauty in my arms and said, 'she's the one.' From that day forward, I knew my goose was cooked."

Grace opened and closed her mouth several times, trying to think of something to say. Why did he have to be so damned charming and handsome!

"Listen, baby girl, you're it for me. It. There is no one else in this world I want to spend my life with. Now, I know you have some things to work through, and I understand that. I'm not going anywhere, Grace; no fucking where I need to be other than right here. When you decide it's more you want, then we get married. Until then, we live in the apartment upstairs."

"Tomorrow. Tomorrow, we're going to be picking out colors and appliances for the house." She looked at him, shocked once again, staring at his handsome face. Tears were swimming in her eyes, and she could only shake her head.

"I love you, Ghost, Eric. I love you like nothing I ever thought possible. Sometimes, I look at you, and I get this pain in my chest like it's too good to be true; it's all a sick joke, and you're going to disappear at some point."

"Baby, I'm not going anywhere. This is not a joke. You are mine, and I am yours, yours, baby girl, forever." He leaned over and kissed her as Angelo placed the dessert on the table.

"Enjoy and congratulations!" he said, smiling at the couple.

"Eric, I noticed some signs for a fall festival next weekend. Do you think we could go? I mean, I love this time of year, all the colors and the smells. It's my favorite time of year. I want to talk to George about doing something big for Thanksgiving. Is that okay?"

"Honey, we'll talk about the festival. I need to make sure some things are taken care of before I agree to that, but as for Thanksgiving, fuck, yea, baby, do it up right."

"Thank you, Ghost. Now, would you mind telling Doc and Zulu that it's okay for them to sit inside the coffee shop across the street so they're not freezing?" Now it was Ghost's turn to be shocked. Opening and closing his mouth like a fish out of water, he could only stare at Grace as she laughed. An Army Ranger and a former SEAL operative sighted by a forty-one-year-old restaurant manager.

Dinner was everything Grace hoped it would be. Conversation, great food, wonderful company, and a chance to take a breath outside the gates of the club. The intimacy of the restaurant made things easier for her, and Ghost was more than comforting. As they rose from the table, Angelo gave her a big hug and held out her coat.

Ghost gripped her fingers between his and moved to the front of the restaurant. As they made their way down the small Main Street of their little town, he spotted Zulu and Doc on the other side of the street and nodded. As they approached the truck, something distracted Ghost just long enough for him to lose his link with Grace's fingers.

In the moments that followed, he truly believed his life would come to an end because he was certain hers would end.

"I have you now, you fucking cunt!" yelled Kyle. Kyle gripped Grace by the hair, a knife digging into her throat, a small trickle of blood already weaving down her throat. From across the street, Zulu and Doc saw the interaction and moved swiftly to take position.

"Let her go, man. This won't end well for you," said Ghost.

"I love you," said Grace, staring at the handsome face of her hero.

"Shut the fuck up! You don't love him. You don't know how to love; you've never loved anyone!"

His body odor was so bad Grace fought back the bile rising in her throat. She smiled at Ghost, who was swiftly losing his shit. Then, as if in slow motion, Grace dug her heel into Kyle's instep. He released her hair, and she turned, pointing the small .38 that Ghost was going to show her how to shoot with. She was pointing it straight at Kyle.

Nothing seemed to move in those moments. The wind seemed to stop. The traffic didn't seem to move. Zulu and Doc seemed in slow motion. Everything stopped... except Grace, who was smooth as molasses.

"I've loved more than you will ever imagine. Go to hell, you son-of-a-bitch." She squeezed the trigger, hitting him in the chest. Then again and again and again. Until Ghost gripped her wrist, lowering the weapon. "You'll never touch me again."

"Baby girl," he said through tears, "baby, look at me, Gracie, look at me." She turned to look up into the most wonderful blue eyes, filled with love, and fear, and concern.

"It's done. It's done," she whispered. Doc immediately started to check on Grace as the crowd gathered. Angelo came out of the restaurant and ran toward them.

"I've called the sheriff, Ghost." Ghost could only nod as he held Grace against his chest, rocking her back and forth.

"I'm okay, Eric. I'm okay. He's dead. He's gone. I've avenged my parents, my daughters. I did it. Me." Ghost couldn't help but shed tears for Grace. She would need to deal with the shootings in the future, but for tonight, she had given herself a sense of peace.

CHAPTER TWENTY-SEVEN

"I think I have everything I need, Grace, Ghost," said Sheriff Webb. "There were enough witnesses, and the cameras all can attest to the fact that it was self-defense. You did well, young lady."

Grace nodded but never lifted her head from Ghost's chest.

"Can we leave now?" asked Doc.

"Yea, boys, you can leave. If I need anything further, I'll come out to your place, but this seems pretty cut and dry. He had no immediate family, and he was a fugitive wanted for murder. I doubt if anyone will make any noise about this one."

"Thanks, Sheriff," said Zulu, shaking his hand.

Zulu and Doc followed Grace and Ghost in their truck. The short drive to the barn seemed like twelve hours tonight. By the time they walked inside, the club was full of people enjoying an evening meal. All eyes of the MC turned toward them as they entered, having received frequent text messages and updates from Doc.

"Gracie? Gracie girl, are you okay?" asked Gunner.

"Is she okay? Is she okay?" asked Ghost. "Forty fucking years taken off my life tonight. Forty fucking years!" he yelled. Grace watched him pacing in front of the other men.

"Ghost..."

"No! No, none of you get to lecture me, none of you! I almost lost her tonight. That fucking whack job was in plain sight, and we all missed it; fucking spec ops, and we all missed it." He turned to face Grace, her beautiful face staring at him wide-eyed. "You are never fucking leaving this place again. Never!"

"Ghost," she said softly, taking a step toward him, "you know it can't be that way. I had to end this. I knew it would be me. I knew it. I could tell he wasn't in his right mind, and I knew no matter what, you, Zulu, and Doc were there. But no one knew I had that gun on me. I told you I wanted to kill him, and I did. I took the gun from your dresser. I put it in my coat pocket. I needed to feel that sense of security.

"Now, I don't ever want to have to do that again. I will if I'm forced, but I don't want to, ever. I felt satisfaction in ending his life, but I don't want that ever again." She touched his cheek, kissing his lips. "I love you, Ghost. I'm free now. I don't have to worry about him coming after me any longer. I don't have to fear going outside or seeing a stranger in the corner. I'm free."

"Baby girl..."

"I'm free to say 'yes,'" she said, smiling. He looked at her, confused, and her smile grew wider. "Yes, Ghost, yes, I will marry you. Yes, I will be your wife."

The smiles of their friends filled the circle, and Ghost still looked like he was in shock until he moved forward, kneeling. He pulled a dark velvet box from his pocket and grinned up at her. Opening the box, he placed the two-carat diamond solitaire on her finger.

"You had this all planned," she said, smiling.

"I sure as fuck didn't plan you killing Kyle, baby girl, but I did plan to ask you to marry me." Ghost stood, still holding her hand. "Say it again, Gracie girl, say it again."

"Yes," she whispered against his lips.

"She said yes!" he screamed, spinning her around. Grace laughed and then felt the bubble of wine burning in her stomach again. Closing her eyes, she patted his shoulder so he would put her down. "You okay, baby?"

"Yea, yea, the wine didn't agree with me tonight, that's all." The entire MC hugged her, congratulating Ghost. When it was done, they retired to their apartment, wrapped in one another's arms.

"It's done, Gracie girl. You're mine."

CHAPTER TWENTY-EIGHT

"So, we meet with Ivan and then maybe Anton, right?" Whiskey nodded. "So, is this guy like richer than Midas or something?" asked Ace.

"You should know, asshole. You're the one that pulled all his information," said Whiskey.

"Yea, yea, I know. I'm just nervous. Dude, this guy is fucking whacked. I'm not sure we're doing any better talking to him than we were talking to Scar. According to the information I gathered, and it was verified by the bureau boys, he's the second oldest son of Vladimir Krevnyv. Cold war general with a penchant for torturing people to get what he wanted. The oldest son served in the old Russian Red Army. He was killed in Afghanistan during the war with the Russians."

"Sucks," said Whiskey as he took a sip of his namesake, watching the doors of the hotel lobby.

"Yea. Anton took over for his father ten years ago. The old man had millions already in business holdings – legitimate shit too – shipping, oil, hotels, everything. But Anton thinks he has a better way to make money and starts working with the Russian mob. Before long, he's in so deep he can't get out.

"Now, most people with his money would find a way to disappear. Our boy Anton has balls the size of grapefruits. He decides he's just going to take out every member of the mob, and he does it. Paying off their own people, hiring mercenaries, anything to get rid of his issue. He makes his way to the states two years ago to work a deal with the Mexican cartel on running drugs, guns, and women."

"Christ! What a piece of shit," mumbled whiskey.

"Yea, piece of shit with millions in the bank, millions more in merchandise, and a thirst for more. His one weakness? He has a daughter of his own. She's twenty-two and a stone-cold fox, brother." Ace held up his phone, showing Whiskey the picture.

"Holy shit, that piece of garbage spawned that gorgeous creature?" The woman in the photo was walking into a restaurant. Her long, lean legs stretched beneath a skintight pencil skirt, and body-hugging tank top covered her large breasts, which by all accounts were not secured with a bra. An expensive handbag was slung over her shoulder, sunglasses framing a beautiful face. Long mahogany waves of hair graced her back, touching the gorgeous ass partly facing the camera. Yea, his dick stirred. He'd admit it.

"Yep. She's currently studying at Georgetown, pre-law of all the bullshit. According to the bureau, Katarina doesn't care much for her father. She tolerates the monthly visits from him and the dinners upon request, but that's it."

"Do they believe her?" asked Whiskey.

"They're inclined to believe her because she turned in her own brother and mother, without her dad knowing. Seems Mama and son were doing their own side business of selling babies on the black markets."

"What a fucked-up family."

"You can say that again. Katarina found a way to get to the bureau who was able to catch them in the act. I'm not sure if Daddy knows or not. His frequent visits with her might be a case of keeping his enemies close. Either way, he's fiercely protective of her. She might be the way we get to him if we need an ace in the hole."

"I don't want any part of kidnapping a young woman who already is in neck-deep. I think, for now, we get a feel for what he knows about Scar and the Warriors." Ace nodded at Whiskey and closed his laptop. They'd both removed their kuttes, leaving them in the hotel room. Not this hotel because this hotel was easily a grand a night, and that shit was not worth it. No, they were staying at a cheaper hotel on the other side of the Potomac.

"That's Ivan," said Whiskey, nodding his head toward a man who'd just entered the hotel lobby.

They both remembered the man from their time in-country. At the time, he was working with the SAS, and they'd met on several missions. He spoke Russian, English, and Farsi fluently and had a keen mind for strategy. He was small and wiry but handled himself well on multiple occasions.

"Ivan," said Whiskey, extending a hand, "nice to see you, brother."

"Nice to see you both as well," he said, smiling. "I trust Ghost is doing well." They nodded and looked behind the man.

"Is that him?" asked Ace.

"Yes. He sent me in first to be sure you were legitimate and alone. He thinks I'm working with him to help broker deals with the cartels. If I say anything offensive to either of you, I'll apologize now. Just go with it."

The man entering the lobby with three beefy, no-necked men following him was average height, with a somewhat bulky build. Not the kind of body built by work, but rather the kind built by eating too much meat and drinking too much vodka.

His suit was impeccably cut, and even from far away, they knew he probably smelled like expensive cologne. His silver hair was slicked back against his head. His watch, covered in diamonds, was probably worth more than the average soldier made in a year. On his feet were some sort of exotic skinned shoes. One gold signet ring was on his left hand.

Whiskey stood, and Ace followed, waiting for Anton to approach. As he stepped up on the raised bar area, he turned to the three bodyguards saying something neither could hear.

"Mr. Krevnyv, this is Whiskey and Ace," said Ivan.

"Yes, you must be the gentlemen from Steel Patriots, the motorcycle gang." His voice was deep with just a hint of a Russian accent. "Where is my shipment?"

Okay then, fucker wants to jump right into that shit, then let's do it.

"First off, Mr. Krevnyv, it's a club, not a gang, and your shipment was returned to their families, sir. They were forced into that truck and taken against their will." He smiled at Whiskey as if to say, 'do you think me a fool?'

"Most of my shipments like this one are… not voluntary," he said. "I'm sure you're aware that in business, we often have to do things we don't like, but supply and demand dictate our businesses sometimes."

"Yes, sir, we understand. But imagine how you would feel if that were your daughter," said Whiskey. Ivan started to speak, but Anton held up a hand, quieting the other man.

"Do not speak of my daughter – ever – do I make myself clear?" he said.

"Clear. Just trying to make a point. Look, Mr. Krevnyv, you're a businessman, and so are we. We help people find their lost children, and we're good at it. It's why people hire us. Now, we were hired to find those girls, and we did our job. Something we're all very proud of. The Warriors were hired to get your shipment to you, and they failed. I'd say this is a simple case of one organization being profoundly better than another one. We have nothing against you. We do, however, have plenty against the Warriors."

Anton eyed the man suspiciously. This man did not speak like an outlaw biker. He spoke with intelligence and authority, and that spelled danger.

"You do not speak like a biker," he said matter-of-factly.

"And how does a biker speak, Mr. Krevnyv? Never mind, that's rhetorical. I'm an educated man, sir. The fact that I like riding a motorcycle has nothing to do with my education. Now, if you prefer I speak like Scar, I can do that, although it pains me." Whiskey waited for a response, and when it didn't come, he continued. "As I said, our beef is with the Warriors, not you."

"This is not my business," he said dismissively.

"But it is, sir. If you continue to do business with the Warriors, I can promise you that they will fuck up so badly it will end up in your lap. Their president, Scar, is hooked on the drugs he sells and has already murdered two young women who were under his protection. He's completely lost touch with reality, and if you continue to do business with him, it will come back on you. I guarantee it."

"What is this?" he asked, waving a hand in the air. "Are you trying to get his business? Is that what this is about?"

"Sir," said Ace, sitting on the edge of his seat, "we have no desire to take over his businesses. We want nothing to do with illegal business dealings. We stop drugs, guns, and the transportation of women and children. That won't change. We are only trying to help you here, even though we disagree with your idea of trade. You're angry we stopped your shipment, and I wish I could tell you we're sorry, but we're not."

Anton's face turned a soft shade of purple, his jaw working back and forth in anger. Ivan wasn't sure what would happen, but he was pretty certain his friends might die in this hotel lobby.

"All we're saying is this, if you continue to do business with the Warriors, we will interfere. If you take your business elsewhere, we'll stay away." Anton raised an eyebrow at the men seated across from him. These Americans had big balls; he'd give them that, but no one dictated to him. Although, they were making a good point. If the fool, Scar, messed up, and it blew back at him, it could create more problems than he needed.

"What are you saying? You're saying if I do business with someone other than the Warriors, you won't interfere in my shipments any longer?" he glanced in their direction, his eyes traveling from one face to another, then down casually at his fingernails.

"If they pass through our territory, we will interfere. I won't lie to you. The Warriors took your money, spent it on drugs, sold those drugs, and then used some for themselves to have a little party. It's them that owes you money, not us. All we're asking is that you stop doing business with them. Scar is using you, Mr. Krevnyv. He's telling the cartel, the mafia, hell, even the Chinese that you're his client. He's using your name to drum up more business for the Warriors. I would think a man like you wouldn't appreciate your name being thrown around like that."

Anton rubbed his beefy fingers over his face, twisting and contorting his lips as he took in the information from the bikers. He knew of their reputation and knew that they were a legitimate business, but he couldn't afford to just let this go. He also couldn't afford to have them interfering further in his business dealings. People would be looking in his direction for retribution. He could not show weakness.

"And how do I save face in this? I have a reputation to uphold," he asked quietly.

"Simple," said Whiskey. "We deliver Scar and his closest advisors to you within two weeks' time. What you do with them is your business, but after that, we'll give you the addresses of three warehouses that we know of that they have stockpiled with drugs and weapons. You clear the warehouses – keep the merchandise. We'll blow them. You can tell your... colleagues they belonged to us."

Anton looked in the direction of Ivan as if wanting some sort of confirmation that the deal was a good one. Ivan gave a small shrug as if he didn't give a shit one way or another.

"Alright. I won't run my shipments through your territory again. I want Scar and five of his men – I don't care which ones – five in my custody by the end of the month. Call Ivan, and he will let me know when you're ready for us to clear the warehouses. The inventory should compensate for my losses of the women."

"Girls," said Ace. "Just to be clear, they were girls, not women." Anton let a slow, malicious smile slip from his lips.

"This one has balls, yes?" he said, smiling at Ivan.

"Fucking Americans, they're all cowboys," said Ivan, grinning at Anton. Whiskey and Ace said nothing, just staring at the men.

"We have a deal, gentlemen. Next time, I wish to meet this Ghost. He is talked about much." Whiskey only nodded as the man left the table. Ivan stood for a moment, waiting until Anton and his goons were out the front door.

"You guys are fucking crazy, you know that, right? Anyone else he would have cut your throats in the middle of this fucking five-star hotel." Whiskey shrugged and chugged the rest of his drink. "Let me know when you have Scar and his weasels."

Ace shook his friend's hand and nodded. They watched the other man leave the hotel and then sat back down in the leather chairs. Neither said anything for several moments. Then Whiskey spoke up.

"I fucking hate Russians."

CHAPTER TWENTY-NINE

Grace turned, looking around the huge open floor plan, and smiled. Ghost talked about the house he was building on the property, but she never dreamed it would look like this. It wasn't huge, three bedrooms and two bathrooms, but the floor-to-ceiling windows facing the forested bluffs created a spectacular view of the land that Ghost inherited. Views for miles and miles created picture postcard-like vistas.

The light Ash wood floors were covered in dust, but she could imagine making those floors shine, light from the windows reflecting off their clean surfaces. The stone fireplace occupied the entire wall next to the windows. She pictured the two of them curled up in front of the flickering flames for the rest of their lives.

"Gracie? What do you think, baby?" he asked, wrapping his arms around her from behind.

"It's beautiful, Eric. It's so beautiful. I can't believe this. We'll be close enough to the club that we can walk to it for work or meetings, and yet we're far enough away to have privacy. I love it." She turned in his arms and kissed him as he lifted her off her feet.

"A few of the other guys are building here. Zulu and Gunner bought townhomes that are in the process of being built about eight miles from here. It was time. Living in the apartments is great, but they're small. It's ideal for the younger guys, but I think the older we get, the more space we want."

Grace nodded, walking around the space once more. She stared out the big expanse of windows, and a sudden feeling of panic overcame her.

"Will... will there be security on the house?" she asked.

"Baby girl, we will have fucking awesome security, but remember, it's on our property, so it will still be fenced in and secure." She nodded again and buried her face into the warmth of his chest. A knock on the door alerted them of their guest as he entered with an armload of materials.

"I hope I'm not interrupting," he said, smiling at the couple.

"Hey, Grant," said Ghost, stepping forward with an outstretched hand, "not at all. Let me introduce you to my fiancée, Grace. Grace, this is Grant Zimmerman, the contractor we're using."

Grace looked up at the man in front of her. He was taller than Ghost but lean, almost thin, like a basketball player. He appeared to be in his late-twenties, a boyish grin filling his face.

"Hello, Grant," she said quietly. "You look very young to be a contractor."

"Well, thank you," he said, laughing. "I suppose I am young. I'm twenty-eight, but my family has been building homes in this area for fifty years. My grandfather knew Eric's dad. I used to play on the old farm here when I was little. Ghost was overseas then, but I'd hear stories from his dad about his badass Navy SEAL son and wanted to be him."

Ghost gave a small grin and looked down at Grace, blushing.

"So why didn't you?" he tilted his head, looking at the pretty woman. "I mean, why didn't you become a SEAL."

"Oh, well, two reasons. One is that I'm six-foot-six, and that would be challenging, not impossible, but challenging. The other reason is I lost about fifty percent of my hearing in my left ear due to an infection when I was a child. They wouldn't take me. So, here I am."

"I'm sorry about that, but if this is any indication of your talent, I'd say you followed the right path."

"I like her," he said, smiling at Ghost. "Okay, what do you say we get down to business? I need for you guys to choose your paint colors today and the tile for the bathrooms, as well as the kitchen. I've brought several samples based on what I thought might work for the space."

They spent the next hour setting samples on the different spaces and discussing colors. In truth, Ghost couldn't have given a fuck as long as it got finished, but he knew that Grace cared, and so it mattered to him. When they finished, Grant packed everything up in his truck.

"I should have the tile delivered by next week and installed by the week after. With any luck, we should have everything completed and the final inspections and walk-through done by mid-December."

"Oh, that would be amazing!" said Grace. "I can already picture having a huge Christmas tree in front of that window."

Grant nodded, smiling at the woman.

"It would be beautiful for sure, Miss Grace. I'll see y'all soon."

Grace wrapped her arms around Ghost's waist, and buried her face in his chest, inhaling the scent she now knew so well. The smell of man, motor oil, leather. The scent that brought her comfort instead of fear. She took another deep breath and suddenly felt bile rising in her throat. Stepping back, she swallowed hard.

"Gracie? Baby girl, are you okay?" he asked.

"Yea, of course, I just felt a little nauseous for a moment. It's all good now." She looked around the room again. "It's going to be so beautiful, Eric."

"It is, baby. Remember, if you want us to go pack up your house, we can do that." She nodded and looked out the back windows once again. This was a view she was going to enjoy.

"I think... I think maybe we should at least clear the house out and get everything into storage. Do you think we can hire someone to do that for me?" she asked.

"We can do anything you wanna do, baby. I can arrange to sell the house for you, and we'll get everything in storage up this way." She nodded again, clinging to him once more. Ghost's phone chirped, and he looked down to see that Whiskey and Ace had returned from DC. He was anxious to hear what they had to say, but he also didn't want to rush this moment with Grace.

"It's okay," she said, smiling. "I know you probably need to get back to business. I do have a question, though. What about furniture? I mean, you don't have much in your apartment, and there is a lot of space here to fill. I have some furniture I guess... I guess I could use some of it. I don't know." She faded off into thin air, her voice barely heard.

"Honey, whatever you want, we'll buy, anything. If you want to use some of your stuff, we'll use it. If not, we buy new stuff. It's that simple." He pulled her towards the door and reached for the handle. Before he could open the door, Grace turned his body, leaning him against the massive door, her hand gliding up his sides to cup his face.

"I love you," she whispered against his lips. She slid her tongue along his opened mouth and tasted him, lifting her leg as she did. He tugged her toward him. Ghost gripped her ass cheeks and lifted her, wrapping her legs around his hips. He turned, slamming her against the door. His already stiff cock rubbed against her warm wet core.

"Fuck, baby girl, you're so fucking hot," he murmured.

"I need you, Eric, I need you..." she panted, desperate to feel his flesh against hers.

Ghost set her feet on the floor and unzipped her jeans, yanking them to the floor, pulling her shoes off with them. Opening his own zipper, he pulled his rigid cock from his boxers, shoving the jeans to his ankles. He picked her up once again, sliding her down his long hot shaft, feeling her warm slick

pussy drench him.

"Oh... oh God! Eric... yea, baby... more..."

"Fuuuuckkk... Gracie girl... yes, honey... yes... rock those hips, baby..." Grace moved back and

forth, up and down, as his strong hands held her to him, ramming her back into the door. She felt the

waves of pleasure start from her head, moving down... down...

"Eric! I'm cumming, baby!" she yelled.

He couldn't even speak. He just growled into her mouth, their tongues dancing as he fisted her

hair – pulling her head back. He powered into her, filling her with his desire and lust. Ghost trailed

kisses down her throat and neck, shivering with the last remnants of juice dripping between their

bodies.

"Fuck, baby girl, that was hot," he said, lifting her from his semi-hard cock.

"Our first time in our new house," she smiled, pulling on her jeans. "I can't wait for many more,

especially on our new kitchen counters, and the shower, and the bathroom counters, and..." her voice

faded off as she walked toward the waiting truck, and he could only smile.

How the fuck did I get so lucky?

CHAPTER THIRTY

By the time Grace and Ghost entered the club, Whiskey, Ace, and several other guys were eating lunch. Grace immediately moved to give them both 'welcome home' hugs, and the men smiled at her as she took a seat next to Zulu and Ghost.

"How was your trip?" asked Grace casually. Whiskey looked at Ghost, who shot him a stare that said, 'don't say a fucking word.'

"It was good, Gracie girl, but more importantly, how are you?" he asked sincerely, quickly changing the direction of the conversation.

"I'm good. Really, guys, I'm doing as well as can be expected, as my sweet doctor keeps telling me." She gave a quick wink and smiled toward Doc. "We just came from picking out colors and tile for the house. It's going to be beautiful. I can't wait to celebrate Christmas in the new house."

"Sounds amazing," smiled Ace, feeling a little bit of envy for his friend.

"Speaking of which," said Grace, "Thanksgiving is only a few weeks away, and I want to plan a big dinner, so let me know if you're going to go home to see parents or siblings. I want to make sure I have an accurate count for George." The men all looked up, somewhat shocked but smiling in her direction.

"What? Do you guys not celebrate Thanksgiving?"

"We do, baby girl, but it's usually just casual," said Ghost, kissing her forehead.

"Oh, well, we could do casual, but, well, I was thinking, I mean, you're all like a family, and families should celebrate in a big way, so I was going to push tables together and do dinner here in the club for everyone."

"I think it sounds amazing, Grace," said Doc. "One thing you got wrong, though. We are a family, but you're included in that. You need to start saying 'we are family' not 'you all are family.' Understand?" Grace nodded, smiling at the big man.

"How are the twins?" she asked.

"They're assholes, is what they are. I swear to fuck, I hope they never get laid up again. They get mischievous, like mean and nasty mischief. Those little shits put Tabasco sauce in the shower gel in the gym shower rooms. I had three guys come to me all at once with burning, itching eyes and dicks... uhhhh... sorry, Gracie. I wanted to kill the little fucks."

Grace laughed, covering her mouth as she did.

"Sorry. I know that must have been uncomfortable, but I tried to tell you guys they're really just like little kids."

"Yea, well, they're out of quarantine now, so they're fair game for payback." Grace nodded, seeing Eagle behind the bar looking sheepishly at the group. She waved in his direction, and he gave her a sweet nod back.

"Okay, well, I know you all have a lot to talk about, so I'll head upstairs. I'm on the bar tonight between five and ten. I'll see you then." She stood, kissing Ghost as she did. He watched her ass sway back and forth as she headed to the private quarters, smiling.

"You're a lucky prick, boss," said Zulu.

"Fucking right, I am," he grinned. "So, what about Krevnyv?"

"He was a real piece of work," said Ace. "Came in like he owned the fucking city. Three bodyguards the size of boulders. Ivan came in first to warn us and was spot on. We convinced him that the Warriors were at fault. Whiskey told him how out of control Scar is and that sooner or later, his shit would bounce back to him."

"Good, nice work. What did he say?" asked Ghost.

"He agreed to keep his shipments out of our territory. He also agreed that appropriate payback would be to give him Scar and five of his associates within two weeks. He also wants what he has stockpiled in the warehouses. He'll blow the warehouses and spread the word that they belonged to us, claiming that's what happens when he's double-crossed."

"Fucking prick!" growled Whiskey.

"He was that," said Ace, "but he got very, very testy when we brought up his daughter. I think we keep that little nugget tucked away for future use." Ghost nodded, although he didn't want to ever use an innocent woman to get what he needed.

"Okay, then we have a plan. We need to figure out a way to get Scar and five of his worst offenders in one place. Tango? Get with Ice and Axe. See if we can figure out a schedule that will allow us to get them all in one spot. Zulu? Do some recon, brother. Watch Scar, and see if you can find a pattern with him. Take Blade with you." Zulu stood, nodding at Blade as they headed back to the private quarters.

"Once we have the intel from Zulu and Blade, we'll make a plan to take them and hand them over to Anton. We need to make sure we give protection to Ice and Axe, make it look like they blew with the warehouses if need be. The rest can go their own ways, but we will end the Warriors after this."

The others all nodded in his direction.

"Are we just going to hand over drugs and guns to Anton?" asked Doc.

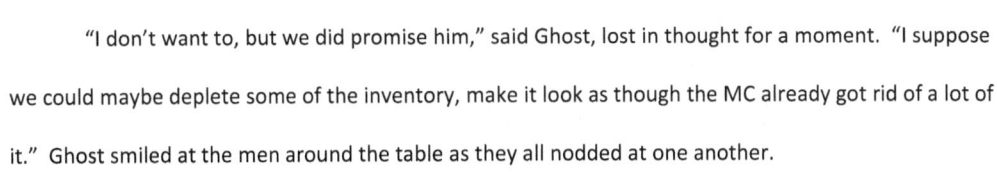

"I don't want to, but we did promise him," said Ghost, lost in thought for a moment. "I suppose we could maybe deplete some of the inventory, make it look as though the MC already got rid of a lot of it." Ghost smiled at the men around the table as they all nodded at one another.

"Fuck, yea," said Gunner. "I say we take weapons we may want to use and leave the rest... perhaps without firing pins," he grinned.

"Oh, man," laughed Ace, "that's gonna be fucking awesome."

"Okay, you all have your orders. Let's end this shit."

CHAPTER THIRTY-ONE

Grace moved around the small apartment, bending to pick up the dirty laundry. She wobbled, dizziness overtaking her, and stood carefully, leaning back on the chair. What the hell was going on with her? Wine that made her sick. Dizziness, bouts of nausea. The last time she felt like this was...

No, no, it couldn't be true. She was told... she was told she couldn't... no. She picked up her phone and dialed the number of her old gynecologist. It was a Saturday, but they were old friends, and Melanie always said she could use her private number.

"Grace! Oh my gosh! I'm so glad you called. I heard what happened, honey. I'm so sorry I didn't reach out to you... I just didn't..." her voice trailed off.

"It's okay, Mel. Believe me, I wasn't in a good place to talk to anyone for those first few months."

"How are you now, honey?" she asked.

"I'm good, Mel, better than good. I found a place where I feel safe, protected. I've fallen in love again." She said, smiling into the phone.

"Oh, honey, I'm so happy for you. You deserve this, Grace."

"Yea, that's kind of what I'm calling about. Do you remember the letter you sent me telling me that I was not able to have any more children?"

"Any more children? Grace, I never sent you a letter like that."

"Wh-what? No... I remember... the girls were like four or five, and I wanted another baby. Kyle... Kyle opened the letter and said he was sorry, but I couldn't have any more children."

"No, no, that's not right. I sent you a letter saying that your hormone levels were fine, your x-rays and ultrasound were fine. You were perfectly healthy." Melanie paused, and Grace could hear her pecking away on her keyboard. "Give me a minute, sweetie. I'm checking hospital records... just between you and me."

"I can't believe this. All this time, I thought..."

"I found it. Kyle had a vasectomy, honey. It would have been around that time. I'm so sorry, Grace."

"No, no, don't be sorry. I'm glad I didn't have any more children. I just wish I'd known."

"Grace? Do you think you're pregnant, honey?" asked Melanie.

"I think so," she whispered. "I mean, I haven't done a test yet, but all the symptoms. Oh God! Mel! Mel, I'm too old. I'm forty-one; I'm too old to have a baby." Melanie laughed on the other end of the line.

"Obviously, you're not too old, honey, and although there are some risks for women of your age having children, it's not unheard of, and most have normal, healthy pregnancies. My recommendation is you find yourself a good gynecologist in the area and get an appointment as soon as possible."

"Right. Right, as soon as possible."

"Grace, it's going to be okay, sweetie. Call me if you need any recommendations, and I'll be happy to give it to you, okay?"

"Yea..."

"Will he be happy? Your new man? Do you think he'll be happy?"

"I don't know… oh shit… I need to tell him. Thanks, Mel… I'll let you know if I need anything." Grace didn't even wait for a response. She simply hung up the phone and headed out the door. As she made her way down the stairs and through the steel doors, she spotted Ghost standing with Whiskey, Doc, and Gunner. He turned to smile at her, and then a look of concern filled his face.

"Gracie, baby girl, are you okay?" he asked, holding her hands. She shook her head, biting down hard on her lip.

"Grace? Are you sick, honey?" asked Doc. She shook her head again and then tilted it sideways, nodding and then shaking again.

"Baby girl, you're scaring the shit out of me. What's wrong?"

"I hope nothing. I didn't know. I didn't know that Kyle lied to me," she said in a whisper.

"That he lied to you about what, Grace?" asked Gunner.

"I think… I'm pretty sure I'm pr-pregnant." Ghost looked at her, a serious expression crossing his face. "I swear to you I didn't know. I thought I couldn't get pregnant. He lied to me. He falsified a letter from my doctor. I just spoke to her. Oh God! I'm so sorry, Eric, I didn't know. I'm so s-sorry…"

"Sorry? What the fuck are you sorry for?" he asked, smiling down at her. "I'm happy as fuck! I couldn't be happier if you'd told me we'd won the lottery. I'm fucking thrilled!"

"Really? You're not mad…"

"Mad? Gracie, baby girl, I fucking love you. You are mine and this," he said, placing his hands over her belly, "this little guy or girl is ours. Ours, baby. I'm gonna be a daddy… a fucking daddy!"

Grace laughed and hugged him, feelings of excitement, fear, and dread filling her body. She was forty-one years old. It was going to be a tough pregnancy, and she could only pray everything went well.

What if she had twins again? Oh Lord, what would they do with twins? Could she handle that? Would she be able to look at them and not be sad?

Definitely, this was her new beginning. It was as if her entire body were enveloped in warmth and sunshine. She could have sworn she heard her parents' voices in her ears, her daughters touching her shoulders. It would all be okay.

"I love you," she whispered to Ghost.

"I love you too, Mama," he said, grinning.

CHAPTER THIRTY-TWO

Grace and Ghost confirmed the pregnancy with not one but three pregnancy tests and easily found a local doctor, making an appointment for the following week. He argued with her about working the bar shift, but she insisted that staying busy and active would help both her and the pregnancy.

It didn't go without notice by the waitresses that every time she had to pour red wine, Grace turned a little green.

"Grace, why don't you just set the bottles within reach, and I'll pour them," said Shelly, one of the three full-time wait staff.

"That might be a good idea. No one wants to have puke in their wine glass," she grimaced.

"No," laughed Shelly, "I'm sure they don't." Shelly was in her mid-fifties, a grandmother of two teenagers whom she was now raising. She worked every shift they would give her at the club, and she worked hard. She'd been one of the first people to make Grace feel welcome at the club.

Grace set the bottles of wine within reach for the waitresses and went about her normal duties of pouring beer and mixed drinks. Doc and Ghost were laughing over a basket of wings while Eagle and Hawk talked to two young women near the pool tables. Gunner was laughing about something Ace said, and Gunner was walking in from the private quarters, freshly showered and smiling.

This was her family now. Her crazy dysfunctional family and the little life growing inside her belly would have so many uncles to protect him or her, it would be mind-blowing.

Grace felt the cold air from the front door opening and turned to see the beautiful smile of her red-headed therapist. She grinned and waved as Aubrey moved toward the bar.

"Hi, Grace," said Aubrey.

"Hi, Aubrey! What brings you out tonight?" The woman shrugged her shoulders and let out a long sigh.

"Please call me Bree, and I didn't plan on coming out necessarily. My car broke down about a mile away, and I knew the garage was close. I walked, hoping that maybe I could get a tow."

"Oh, that sucks! Of course," she said, waving at Ghost. He stood and Doc, seeing who Grace was speaking with, followed him.

"Hi, Aubrey," said Ghost.

"Bree," she said, smiling.

"Honey, Bree's car broke down about a mile down the road, and she was hoping we could tow her into the garage."

"You walked?" yelled Doc. Bree looked up at the big man, her face shading a bright pink.

"Yes, I walked," she said defiantly. "I'm capable of walking, Mr… Mr… what was your name again?"

"Doc, my name is Jack Harris, but they call me Doc."

"Are you a doctor?" she asked with arms folded beneath her beautiful full breasts. It only served to emphasize their beauty as the movement pushed them upwards out of her white blouse.

"No. I'm not a doctor. I was a medic while serving as a Ranger and a damned fine one," he ground out. "In the military, they often call medics 'doc.' The name just stuck with me." Bree wanted to reply something smart but didn't want to offend him. She understood the reasoning for calling him Doc, but she wasn't happy with his attitude.

"Well, either way, I walked, and I need a tow. Is that something you can help me with?"

"You should have called," said Doc, staring down at her. "It's dangerous for a woman to be out at night on these backroads walking. You could have been hit, or kidnapped, or even attacked by a wild animal."

"Oh really!? You are unbelievable. I'm quite capable of taking care of myself, *Jack*," she said, staring up at him. Ghost looked over at Grace, who was grinning ear to ear for some reason. He looked back at Doc, who was now standing with his own arms folded, nearly touching the arms of Bree in front of him. Doc was easily six-foot-five, but Bree was probably five-ten without the heels, so they were a fine match.

He finally cleared his throat, interrupting the moment.

"Well, I'll send someone to pick up your vehicle if you'll just give me your keys, Bree," said Ghost. "I can have someone take you home when you're ready, but why don't you enjoy supper on us tonight." Bree stared straight into the eyes of Doc and then turned slowly, facing Ghost.

"Thank you, Ghost. That's very kind of you," she handed him her keys and then took a seat at the bar to chat with Grace, effectively turning her back on Doc. Ghost pulled him towards the door.

"What the fuck is wrong with you? Why were you trying to antagonize that poor woman?" asked Ghost. Doc ran his hands through his hair, gritting his teeth.

"I-I don't know. It just came out. I was suddenly so angry that she walked all that way by herself, alone in the dark. Fuck! Anything could have happened to her." Ghost looked at his friend and back at the pretty red-headed doctor.

"Well, just be nice. She's important to Grace. I'm going to send the twins to get the car and bring it to the garage. Maybe you could be nice and offer to take her home." Doc nodded, not saying anything but watched as she and Grace casually chatted, laughing as they did. Her beautiful red hair cascaded down her back as she tilted her head in a laugh. Her round ass cheeks perched perfectly on the bar stool.

He groaned, watching her cross one long leg over the other, the fullness of her thighs stretching against the fabric of her blue jeans. She turned sideways, watching the people of the club mill about, the buttons on her white blouse gaping, giving him a perfect view of full round globes of pleasure. His eyes moved upward until they finally rested on her beautiful face. Plump red lips, a pert nose, and hazel eyes... staring straight at him.

Doc blushed slightly, having been caught in the act of staring. But what he noticed more was that the beautiful doctor, Aubrey Collins, Bree was staring at him, and her face was on fire.

CHAPTER THIRTY-THREE

Zulu and Blade watched from the road as bikes filtered into the gravel lot of the broken-down old building. It surprised both men that the majority of the bikes seemed older and in need of repairs, both aesthetically and mechanically. They were trained to hear problems with engines, and most of these guys had some issues. So, where was all their money going from the guns and drugs?

"Fuck," said Zulu, "is that place even safe? It looks like a tinder box ready to go up at any moment."

"That might play well in our favor, brother." Zulu nodded, just watching as the men stood outside in the cold talking, the big double doors open to allow for the smoke to filter into the night sky. The music was so loud both men wondered how anyone heard themselves.

"You see this?" asked Zulu. "I'm counting maybe twenty-five guys; at least a dozen are old as fuck. Two of them shouldn't even be riding anymore; they're walking with canes. I see maybe… two… three… four chicks, and I gotta say, I wouldn't put my dick in them even if I'd just returned from five years in the desert. That's some rough-looking pussy."

"Yea, definitely not the cream of the crop even as club whores go." Blade lowered the night vision goggles to look more closely at the men across the street. They all were packing a pistol or two, tucked into their jeans mostly, which indicated to him they didn't have licenses to carry – no surprise. It also meant that they didn't know what the shit they were doing. Pulling a pistol from your waist wasn't easy and took more time than yanking it from a holster. It could also easily get caught in a belt loop if you didn't know what the hell you were doing.

"There he is," said Zulu, "northwest side of the building. He's got a chick trying to suck him off but looks like the poor thing is struggling with equipment failure." Blade smiled at his friend and then grimaced as he caught sight of Scar gripping the hair of the poor girl on her knees in the gravel.

"Fucking asshole. He's hurting that poor girl and doesn't give a shit." Zulu nodded, watching the man.

"He's fucking shooting up while she's on her knees. Christ, he really has a problem." Blade scanned the front of the building once more. "Looks like two entrances, the main one where everyone is right now, and it looks like there's a backdoor, but that's it."

"If they're sleeping there, I can't imagine what kind of shithole it is," said Zulu. "Almost all of them are using something other than alcohol to get high. I've seen them exchanging smoke, pills. I can't believe these guys can even function any longer."

They watched as two pick-up trucks pulled in, and four younger members stepped out with six young girls following. Zulu's stomach bottomed out as he watched the high school or college-aged girls, their jeans skintight, sweaters showing more than they should. Whistles and catcalls were heard, and he turned to see Blade.

"Fucking fuck nugget! What do we do now?" asked Blade.

"We can't do anything, brother," he growled from deep in his chest. "It's two of us and two dozen of them. Even with them drunk and high, we'd be in a shit ton of trouble." He said nothing for a few minutes and then smiled at his friend.

"Of course, if the police were called, a complaint made that I believe my under-aged daughter is in that building…"

"You are seriously genius, asshole," smiled Blade. Zulu made the call and waited, hearing the sirens coming quickly. As two police cars pulled into the parking lot, the face of Scar was more than a little aggravated. It took two men to pull him back inside while the officers made the young women come out of the building and into the light.

One was half-dressed, clutching her top to her bare breasts, tears streaming down her face. Another was already sporting a bloody lip, but it appeared they were all safe and help was received in time. This time.

But what about next time? What then? What would happen when the next group of girls entered that hellhole, and Zulu and Blade weren't watching?

What?

CHAPTER THIRTY-FOUR

"Is he always such an overbearing Neanderthal jerk? He seemed so nice at your appointment," said Bree. Grace smiled at the woman as she set her burger down in front of her.

"Doc? He's actually one of the most caring, sweet men I've ever met in my life. He's just very protective and especially protective of women. Personally, I think it's kind of nice." Bree nodded at her and then looked back toward the man still staring at her.

"I guess I'm just not used to that. I've been on my own a long time, and believe me, I've never had a man care whether or not I got home okay or worry if I broke down in the middle of nowhere." Grace looked at the beautiful woman, hearing the pain dripping from her words.

"Did you not ever have anyone serious in your life?" asked Grace. Bree said nothing at first, and Grace realized she might be overstepping. "I'm sorry, Bree. That was uncalled for and probably inappropriate."

"No, no, actually, I'd love to talk to another woman like this. I mean, have another woman I can talk to like this. I moved here about a year ago and have a nice patient base of mostly divorcing couples and minor issues, but honestly, there aren't a lot of places for me to meet people my own age."

"Well, I'd love to be your friend, as well as your patient, if you're okay with that. But back to Doc. I think he got overprotective because he likes you."

"Likes me!" squealed Bree a little too loud. "I mean... likes me... what do you mean? I'm nothing special, Grace. If you haven't noticed, the body gods didn't bless me with your leanness. I'm packing more than a few in all the wrong places." She set her burger down, staring at her plate. "And yes, I know I don't help myself, but I love food."

"And you should! Listen, Bree, you know better than anyone that loving yourself is the first step to loving your body. You're a beautiful woman, honey. I mean stunning! You have the face of an angel, and all that red hair is simply gorgeous. I would kill to have your boobs, and don't get me started on your height." Bree blushed, staring at the woman behind the bar.

"Thank you, Grace, truly. I know I'm hard on myself, but it's awfully hard when the world says we should all look a certain way and our genetics say, 'I don't think so.' I mean, you're so petite and gorgeous. You and Ghost make a beautiful couple. Doc... Doc is tall and handsome and..."

"Sexy?" asked Grace with a smile.

"Should you be saying that about your man's best friend?" giggled Bree.

"No, probably not, but I'm not blind. Although," she said, smiling, leaning over the bar, "I did just find out I'm pregnant, so my hormones are probably in overdrive right now. I want to climb Ghost every time I see him."

"Oh my gosh! That's so wonderful! Congratulations! Are you feeling okay?"

"I'm nervous... scared," said Grace. "I mean, I'm forty-one, so this could be a difficult pregnancy, but I feel like maybe this is God giving me another chance at happy. You know what I mean?"

"I do, but I don't think it's 'another chance,' Grace. I think it's just a different chance. You need to remember that you had a beautiful 'happy' for eighteen years. Don't belittle that. You were lucky you had those eighteen years. Now you get a shot at another happy. I don't think there's just one for all of us. I think there are several."

Grace nodded at the woman, smiling. She set the glass down she was cleaning and looked toward Doc, who had a miserable expression on his face.

"Maybe you should try to grab a little happy yourself," said Grace with a big grin, wiggling her eyebrows.

"I don't know, Grace," said Bree. "I should probably get home."

"I'll take you," said the deep voice from behind her. She turned to see Doc standing there, his hands in his pockets, his face with a hint of pink blush on his cheeks. "I mean, if you're okay with that, I'll take you." She nodded and scooted off the barstool.

"Do you have a jacket?" he asked.

"N-no, I left it in the car," she said, raising her hand toward him, "and before you yell at me, I know I should have grabbed it. It was colder than I thought."

"I wasn't going to yell at you. I was going to say you can wear this," he said, handing her a warm hoodie from his hands.

"Thank you."

"You're welcome," he said, staring at her. Grace just looked at the two acting like love-struck teenagers. "Come on, let's get you home."

CHAPTER THIRTY-FIVE

Grace nervously fingered the thin paper gown as she waited patiently for the doctor to return. Why did they have to make these damned gowns so awful-looking and feeling? It rubbed against her skin, crinkling every time she moved. Her breasts felt heavy against her chest, the familiar weight of pregnancy causing her to smile.

They'd been lucky in getting into the only female gynecologist in the area. She was a nice woman, older with kindly gray eyes and a keen sense of intelligence about her. Ghost sat quietly in the chair, just watching Grace, seemingly not nervous at all.

"How are you so calm? What if something is wrong? What if..." he reached for her hands, stilling his own on top of hers. His warm, callused palms rubbing against her soft skin.

"Nothing is wrong, baby, nothing. And if by some fucked up chance there is, we'll deal with it. I'm not going anywhere, Grace. This baby, you and me, we're going to be a family... a happy family." He stood, pulling her against his warm chest. "I love you, baby girl."

The door opened, and the doctor smiled at the couple holding one another. She knew Grace's story and knew they were both concerned about their ages. The truth was she saw women as old as forty-five or forty-six having children nowadays. It wasn't ideal, but it was possible and could be very safe.

"Well, everything is back, and you have a perfectly healthy fetus," said the doctor. "Do you want to know the sex?"

"I... I think I would," said Grace, letting out a relieved breath, staring at Ghost. "I mean, it would help in planning for the nursery and everything we're going to need." He nodded, smiling at the doctor.

"Okay then, you're having a beautiful baby boy."

"A… a boy," smiled Grace. "We're having a son." Tears streamed silently down her face as she looked at Ghost, his face filled with pride and happiness. He hugged her tightly, kissing the top of her head as the doctor smiled at them.

"Now, just take your prenatal vitamins, eat right, get plenty of rest, and all will be well." Ghost stepped forward, wanting to get his say in for the visit.

"Doc, she insists on working. Can I make her stop?" asked Ghost. Grace laughed, tears still streaming down her face. The doctor chuckled and shook her head.

"Mr. Stanton, Grace is capable of working well into her third trimester unless we encounter any problems. Working is good for her and for the baby. Regular exercise is good as well, so is sex," she said with a wink.

"About that," said Grace, blushing, "I'm… I seem to want it more frequently, like desperately. I didn't experience that with my ex-husband." Ghost wanted to puff his chest out proudly but didn't dare.

"Well, dear, did your ex-husband look like that?" she asked slyly. Grace shook her head. "Then there's your answer. I suggest you start taking vitamins as well, young man. I'll see you both in a month."

The doctor left the room, and Grace stood, tearing the paper gown from her body. She looked at Ghost, who was watching every move she made. Holding out her undergarments, he waited for her to take them. Instead, she locked the door and turned toward him.

"I need you now, Ghost," she said, smiling.

"Baby… I… what about…" he couldn't breathe. Fucking hell, this woman wanted him right here, right now. "Fuck it! Come here."

Ghost pulled his stiff cock from his jeans, bending Grace over the exam table, he rammed into her wet pussy, slick with juices. Gripping her hair, he pulled back and ran his finger along her tight hole.

"We need to make use of this, baby girl," he whispered. Using her own juices, he slid a finger inside her.

"Yes... yes, Ghost... do that... I feel so full... make me cum, baby..."

Christ! This woman was so fucking hot she was going to be the death of him. He slid a second finger inside her and heard her gasp, but the effect was exactly what he wanted. The fullness for both of them was beyond imagination. Her tightness cramped around his cock, and he growled, pumping furiously until everything he had spilled inside her.

Grace started to moan, and he placed his hand over her mouth, quieting her. A soft knock on the door broke them both apart.

"Everything okay, Grace?" asked the nurse.

"Oh, yes, I was just having trouble with my jeans. I'll be right out." Ghost grinned at his woman, both of them flushed from sex as she quickly dressed.

"You're hot as fuck, baby girl," he said, kissing her. "Let's get home and do that again."

"Fine," she said, smiling over her shoulder. "But next time, I don't want fingers, Ghost."

He couldn't speak. He could barely move as he followed her out of the exam room. She smiled at the receptionist as she made her next appointment, then held his hand as they made their way to the truck. No more bike until the baby was born.

"You with me, Ghost," she said, grinning at him.

"Yea... with you... no fingers."

CHAPTER THIRTY-SIX

Ghost stared at the room of men as they shared the collected intel. The Warriors were off the rails in more ways than one, and honestly, if it weren't for the shit with Krevnyv, they would have just called the Feds to sweep in and end the bastards. Ghost didn't really give a shit what biker protocol was typically used. They weren't outlaw bikers. In fact, they were the complete fucking opposite. They played by different rules, just rules in general, and ninety-nine percent of the time were probably going against most MCs. He didn't give a shit.

Ice and Axe sat at the end of the table, knowing that just being allowed in the room was a big deal. They knew they'd made a huge mistake after only one day with the Warriors. Both having served with honor, they wanted the feeling of brotherhood once again and thought belonging to an MC would give them some of that once again.

"So, from what we can see, Scar has no pattern to his days," said Zulu. "He gets high, fucks, or at least tries to, sleeps, fights when he has the energy. I assume he shits now and then, but that's all. When he can't get hard, he blames it on the girl and beats the shit out of her. I notice he's doing that a lot out in public."

"Yea," said Axe, "he keeps the front doors open all the time now, not sure why, but my guess is the stench in that place is overwhelming. No one cleans the place, and the guys just don't seem to care anymore. I think he believes he's invincible, and he just doesn't give a shit who sees him any longer. He's been shooting up on the club floor. Everyone sees it."

"The good news," said Ice, "is that three of the older members have split. Told me and Axe that they were retiring and wanted the fuck out. Said if anyone wanted to hunt their old asses down to have at it. Nobody seemed to give a shit, which is good."

"You think they really wanted to retire?" asked Ghost.

"Yea, man, they were all older than sixty-five. One has an old lady, grandkids, shit like that down in Florida. She took off about a year ago, and he finally got the balls to follow. Honestly, I'm happy for him." The men all nodded, understanding what Ice was saying.

"So, no pattern for us to follow at all. Who are the five guys we need to hand over to Anton?"

"My suggestion is, along with Scar, take Spike, Ant, Hammer, Pike, and Digger," said Ice. "Spike and Ant are the closest to him. Both are so jacked on their own shit they can barely move, but he confides everything in them. Hammer and Digger aren't hooked, from what I know, but those bastards are mean and dirty. They enjoy the pain a bit too much. The girl you saw the other night trying to give a blow job to Scar?" Zulu and Blade nodded. "When Scar had his way with her, he tossed her to Hammer and Digger to enjoy. That poor fucking girl was nearly ripped apart. Axe got her to the emergency room before she could die, but she'll never be the same again."

"I want to kill these motherfuckers," growled Zulu.

"Stand in line," said Doc.

"Okay, so we get Scar and those five. But how? Where?" asked Ghost.

"I think we should set a meeting with Scar pretending to be a potential client," said Gunner. "He's trying to branch out to all the big mobs. It would play to his ego. We can pretend that we're part of one of the syndicates and set a meeting. We'll have three guys in suits. Guys he's never seen show up in an SUV. We pick the place. We send our team in well in advance to prep the takedown. He'd have those five with him, right?"

"Yea, in theory, he'd have those five. If not, they'd be easy to pick up one at a time, but that's definitely the hard way to go. Hell, he might show up with more, but you'd get what you want for sure," said Ice.

"Maybe we do this at one of the warehouses," said Ghost. "Tell him we want to see the merchandise, inspect it for ourselves. We can get what we need, get the men, make the call to Anton, and be done with this bullshit."

"It might work," said Ice. "He definitely would want to show what's in those warehouses. He's proud of the stash he has, although the drug stash is dwindling thanks to him and the club using." Ghost raised a brow and stared at the two men.

"You haven't touched the shit, right?" he asked.

"Nothing, Ghost, we promise," said Axe. "It's one of the reasons we wanted out. He pressures guys to try shit. So far, we've been lucky. We volunteer for the shit jobs – road work, clean up, shit like that – so we can avoid the bigger groups."

"Good. Remember what I said. I don't tolerate that shit here." Both men nodded, and he gave a short nod back.

"So, I'm not gonna lie, I'm a little torn about allowing Anton to have his hands on all those drugs and guns. That's shit that will come back to bite us big time. That bastard wouldn't think twice about killing us with the weapons we're handing over to him," said Doc.

"I know what you're saying, brother, but we made the man a deal," said Whiskey. "Now, of course, if they take possession and somewhere down the road, by chance, the feds pulled them over. Well then, I mean…"

"He might be suspicious of that, but we could put trackers in all the crates. If the feds followed the trackers, it might lead them to a bigger stash somewhere away from our territory. I'll ask Ivan if he can contact the DEA, maybe see if they'd be willing to work with us on this," said Ace.

"Alright," said Zulu, "let me play devil's advocate here. Let's just say everything goes to shit. Where would Scar go? Does he have a safe house somewhere or parents, siblings? Anyone that would take him in?"

"It's a good thought, brother," said Ghost. "Ice? Axe?"

"No. No one that we've ever seen or heard of. He killed his own father, and as far as I know, his mother left when he was a kid. I don't think he has any siblings, at least none that I'm aware of. His only friends, if you want to be generous and call them that, are the five guys you're going after. The other guys in the club aren't loyal to him at all."

"My guess is," said Axe, "once you take him and blow the warehouses, they'll scatter. They want out. Hammer… he's the worst. Those girls you saw them bring in the other night? They were brought in by Hammer. He's a nice-looking guy, or so the girls think. But once they get to know him, he's pure ugly. He had two of those girls on the pool table, ripping their clothes off as those cops pulled up. Girls wouldn't have lasted an hour, brother."

"We were ready to jump across the street," said Blade. Ghost nodded, appreciating the sentiment, but he also knew that both men most likely would have died if that had happened.

"Alright, use a burner, and call Scar now. Set the meeting for next Sunday night. Put it on speaker. Gunner? You and Ace handle the call. He's never met either of you, right?" Both men shook their heads as Ice dialed the number.

"Who the fuck is this?" came the slurred response.

"Is this Scar of the Warriors?" asked Gunner in a clear, slightly accented voice. It didn't quite sound Russian but had mixes of German or Slavic hinted in it.

"Yea, who the fuck is this?" he growled.

"This is not the way I would expect potential business associates to discuss future endeavors." Ghost smiled at Gunner.

"Uh, yea, right. Who is this?" he asked again.

"My name is Manfred; that's all you need to know. I represent a very powerful man who has interests on the east coast of the United States, but he's based in Eastern Europe." There was only breathing on the other end of the phone, excitement almost palpable. "Are you there?"

"Yea. Yes, I'm here," he said, suddenly alert.

"Very good. My employer has heard that you have some... supplies for sale. We'd like to see these supplies and take possession as soon as possible. We'll pay your asking price, plus five percent." The men shook their heads, smiling as Gunner planted the seeds of greed. Scar wouldn't be able to refuse the additional cash, and he most likely wouldn't tell the men in the club about it. He'd keep that to himself.

"I have quite a supply, Manfred. Three warehouses full. Are you sure you can handle that kind of inventory?"

"Are you questioning me?" growled Gunner.

"N-no... no, not at all. Just sayin' it's a lot of shit, I mean, a lot of supply. You'll need several eighteen-wheelers to haul it away."

"You let me worry about the hauling of the merchandise. Are you available Sunday at ten p.m. to show the merchandise to myself and my employer?"

"Yea. Yea, sure thing, Sunday at ten."

"Scar, it will just be me, my employer, and one other man. You should have no more than five men with you. If you double-cross us, there will be no end to the wrath brought down on you. If you are honest with us about your supply, I will make you a very wealthy, very popular man. Do I make myself clear?"

"Clear," said Scar.

"Good, text the address to this number. I look forward to meeting you Sunday." Gunner hung up the phone and grinned at the room.

"What the fuck, dude? Did you take acting classes somewhere?" asked Zulu.

"Nope, but did a lot of that shit in the sandbox. You guys know how that goes – good cop, bad cop routine. Okay, let's plan this shit out because I'd like to come home Sunday night."

CHAPTER THIRTY-SEVEN

Grace laughed as she took the last bite of her salad, joking with Bree. It was their third session together, and as promised, Bree met her at the club, enjoying a late lunch and girl chat before their official chat.

"So, you're feeling healthy? No morning sickness?" asked Bree.

"No. I've been really lucky. The only things I seem to suffer from are occasional vertigo, and the red wine smell really sends me over the edge, but other than that, I'm good," said Grace, smiling.

"Cravings?"

"Oh, sweet Jesus, yes!" laughed Grace. "I'm craving pears for some strange reason, vanilla wafer cookies, the smell of leather, and of course Ghost." She wiggled her eyebrows at the other woman, and Bree blushed, laughing at her friend.

"The smell of leather, huh? That's an interesting one. Maybe because you're associating it with him. How are you doing with thinking about starting another family?"

"I don't know. For the most part, I'm excited. I mean, I have a life growing inside of me that's part of the most amazing man I've ever known."

"But…" prompted Bree.

"But I won't lie to you. I do feel some guilt. I mean, it hasn't even been six months since my family was killed, and I'm already moving on. It just doesn't feel normal," she said, tugging at her lip.

"What's normal, Grace? No one knows the answer to that. I've had clients who lost a spouse and moved on within a few weeks. Everyone feels grief differently. We're not in the Middle Ages, and there is no appropriate timeframe for grief. You were divorced, so meeting and falling in love with

Ghost is perfectly alright. The idea of you moving on with your life, without your daughters or your parents is also perfectly normal."

"I know that in my head, and really ninety-nine percent of the time, I'm okay with that. I feel like the girls are looking down on me, smiling that they finally get a baby brother. I don't know. I know that's silly," she said, twisting her napkin.

"It's not silly," said Bree, "it's sweet, and I can't think of a nicer memory to have than that of your daughters blessing you and Ghost and that beautiful child you're carrying." Grace nodded again and smiled, feeling somewhat lighter.

"What about your reactions around men? Are those improving at all?" she asked.

"I think that's improved more than anything. It was like once I knew Kyle was gone, I wasn't afraid anymore. I didn't feel guilty for having to shoot him, but I felt guilt for taking a life, if that makes sense."

"It makes perfect sense," said Bree. "You're a kind woman with high moral character. Killing anyone, even someone who did harm to you and your family, is not something you would take lightly. I think it took tremendous courage for you to do what you did, Grace."

"Thank you. You have no idea how much our talks have helped me, Bree, and it's only been three times. Although, I guess if we count the two lunches and two dinners, you should probably bill me for that time as well," laughed Grace.

"Are you kidding me?!" said Bree. "Those were *my* therapy sessions. I've loved having someone that I can talk to as well, Grace. You're a remarkable woman. Talented, beautiful, kind, I'm lucky to call you friend."

"Speaking of," moaned Grace, staring at Doc standing at the bar, "what gives with you two?" Bree let out a long sigh staring at the sexy man. If her use of batteries for her vibrator were any indication, he was the most frustrating man she'd ever encountered.

"I don't know. I mean, I like him, really, really like him. But I get the sense that he's either not interested or shy. I mean, the night he took me home, he was so sweet and gentlemanly. He walked me to the door, waiting until I unlocked it and turned on the lights, and then shook my hand. He freaking shook my hand!"

Grace winced and looked back over at Doc, who was staring at them.

"When my car was ready, he picked me up, and I gave him back his hoodie. He handed it back to me, and he said, 'I'd love it if you would keep it and wear it now and then thinking of me.' I mean, what man says shit like that?" said Bree in a frustrated voice.

"Wow! I mean, wow. Maybe he is really shy. Look, I know he likes you, and you guys have a lot in common. I mean, both of you are involved in medicine."

"Well, he's not a doctor..." said Bree, regretting the words as she spoke. Grace only smiled and nodded.

"No. No, he's not an M.D., but he is a PA, did you know that?" Bree shook her head. "He earned his master's in nursing while he was a Ranger and then became a PA. He's the guy who patches everyone up here at the club, and I've seen him do it on more than one occasion with people they're helping. He's really remarkable, and believe me, if Ghost weren't such an ass about the man seeing my vagina, I'd let him deliver my child."

Bree broke out in raucous laughter, her face flaming red at the thought of poor Doc having to do an exam on Grace with Ghost standing over this shoulder.

"Listen, I'm no love expert, obviously, but I would just say find something that the two of you have in common and start talking. If nothing else, at least plan on joining us for Thanksgiving here next week."

"Oh, I'd love to," said Bree. "I usually just do some take-out or something, but that sounds fun. What should I bring?"

"How about a dessert or two? These guys love sweets, so believe me, anything goes over big with them." Bree nodded, making a note for herself.

"Okay, sounds great. Now, back to you. Anything else you want to chat about while I'm here?"

"Yes, we need to plan a shopping trip. I need maternity clothes, and despite what my overprotective fiancé thinks, I cannot order them online and expect them to fit. Are you up for a little shopping, maybe Black Friday?"

"Oh girl, now you're speaking my language."

CHAPTER THIRTY-EIGHT

"You ever gonna make a move on that, brother?" asked Tango. Doc said nothing, just continued to stare at the table where Grace and Bree were laughing. "I mean, she's smokin' fucking hot. If you don't, maybe I will."

"You fucking touch her, and I'll make sure you're pissing blood for the next month," he growled. Tango lifted his hands, grinning.

"Whoa, whoa, brother. No need for all that, but you can't just sit back and stare at something that beautiful and not expect that someone isn't going to work up the nerve to touch eventually." Tango watched as Doc continued to stare at the women. He didn't attempt to hide it; he didn't try to turn away. It was as if he didn't care that Bree knew he was staring.

"Okay, asshole, what gives? Why won't you just ask her out?" asked Tango.

"I can't," said Doc.

"You can't? You mean you don't know how?" said Tango, raising an eyebrow. Doc looked at him as if he would come across the bar at him.

"No, I mean, I'm not good at relationships, Tango. You are. I get that. You and Ghost both had reputations with women. I mean, before Grace, he did. I'm just not wired that way." Tango saw the pain on Doc's face and, for the first time, felt badly about teasing his friend.

"Explain, brother."

"Look, I was raised in a very strict religious household. My father didn't even allow my mother to have magazines in the house like *Good Housekeeping*, let alone *Elle* or *Vogue*. He thought the ads showing women shaving their legs or putting deodorant under their arms was provocative and would lead to evil thoughts."

"What the fuck?" said Tango, staring at Doc.

"Yea, what the fuck. Try being a teenager, hormones raging, and your father is trying to convince you that it's only the devil trying to get to you. I was fucking scared half the time and ready to explode the rest of the time. I would wake up after a wet dream, my sheets wet and sticky, and be humiliated. My poor mother had to make sure her arms were covered; her skirts were below her knees, and that she covered her chest."

"Jesus, dude, I'm so fucking sorry. I mean, it's embarrassing for any teenager, but to feel guilty about it sucks. I mean, hell, my mom used to ask me every morning if I had a good dream." Tango shook his head. "She thought she was being a 'cool' mom by asking me about wet dreams. I was so fucking embarrassed. I came home one day and found three Playboy magazines on my bed."

"Man," smiled Doc, "consider yourself lucky. When I went to college, I knew that I'd have to figure things out by myself. I mean, I'm a big guy, not terrible-looking, so girls approached me. Thank God I was studying nursing. I had access to a lot of, well, let's just say, colorful and informative textbooks. But still, I was twenty when I had my first sexual encounter. It was awful. I fired early, all over her legs, and she was pissed."

"Oh fuck," said Tango, trying not to laugh.

"I know. I know. It's funny now, but then I just didn't know what to do. I started watching porn, and believe me, that shit didn't help at all because then I was expecting every chick to drop to her knees and suck my cock. When I joined the Army, I actually listened more to the guys in the barracks. Overseas, well, overseas, as you well know, we get a lot of action, and hence a lot of practice."

"So, I don't get it. You've had a lot of chicks and a lot of practice, but you can't ask her out. Why?" asked Tango.

"I did get a lot of practice, for sex, not for dating or asking a woman out. I've never asked a woman out. Never. I've never had a real date. I've fucked plenty, but it was all pick-ups and one-night stands. I have never dated."

"No shit!" said Tango a little too loud.

"Hey, asshole, not helping," said Doc, staring back at the table.

"Look, man, she likes you. It's obvious, and you like her. Just be yourself, brother. You're a stand-up dude, smart, great shape, kinda good-looking," said Tango, wincing. Doc laughed.

"Yea. Yea, maybe when all this shit with the Warriors is over." Tango nodded.

"Or, maybe before," he said, seeing Bree walk toward them.

"Hi. Umm, it's Tango, right?" she asked.

"That's right, beautiful. Nice to see you again. I'll check you later, Doc," he said, leaving them to stare at one another.

"I hope I didn't chase him off if you two were busy," said Bree.

"Oh. Oh, no, he had work or something," said Doc, fumbling with his words.

"Well, I was... I mean, I wanted to ask you... oh, geez, I'm not very good at this. I have a conference coming up in Toronto in a few weeks. It's the week after Thanksgiving. It's on new theories and techniques to use with victims of trauma and abuse."

"That sounds fascinating... fun, I mean," he said, staring at her. "Well, maybe fun is the wrong word, but I'm sure you'll learn a lot of really great information." Doc rolled his eyes in his mind. He was fucking this up royally.

"Yea. Yea, it should be... fun... I mean, good. I was wondering... I mean, I know what you guys do here... Ghost and Grace told me. So, I was wondering if you might like to come with me. I mean, I have an extra ticket for the conference and..."

"Yes!" he blurted out before she could finish. "Yes, I'd love to join you." She smiled up at him, her face burning with a furious blush.

"Okay then. I'll send you my flight information, and maybe we can be on the same flight. Until then, I'll see you on Thanksgiving." He looked at her curiously. "Oh, umm, Grace invited me for Thanksgiving dinner. I'll see you then." He nodded again and smiled.

"Thanks for asking me, Bree. I'm glad you did." She smiled, laying one of her well-manicured hands on his shoulder.

"Me too," she said with a soft kiss to his cheek. He watched as she exited the club and turned to see Tango, Whiskey, Eagle, and Hawk all smiling at him with big thumbs up. He shook his head and gave them all one finger up.

CHAPTER THIRTY-NINE

Comment [MK]: Obviously Gunner cant stare at Gunner – my fault

Gunner, Ace, and Blade stood in the middle of the club looking like they'd just stepped off Wall Street. All three men shaved their beards off, much to their disappointment, and cut their hair. Fortunately, their tattoos were easily covered by the suits, nothing visible at the necks or on their hands. All the men had suits in case they had to appear in court for cases that they helped on.

"You look like a fucking banker," said Gunner, staring at Ace.

"Fuck you, asshole. Gracie girl said I look nice, and I'll take her word over yours any day of the week." Gunner laughed, hitting his friend lightly on the shoulder.

"Okay, everyone, listen up," said Ghost. "Zulu, Gunner, and Skull have eyes on the property. Zulu said your boy, Hammer, came by the warehouse an hour ago, walking around the property looking for any signs that someone was already there. Said he was a fucking amateur." Ice nodded.

"Yep, that would be him, but pay attention. He's a fucking brutal amateur." Ghost gave a quick nod.

"Once Hammer left, Zulu and the boys got busy planting tracking devices and removing the firing pins. Our boys are already out of the other warehouses, tracking devices planted. Anton has been notified, and he and his boys are nearby waiting for our word."

"Eagle, Hawk, and Axe will stay here with Grace, watching the club. We're slow on Sunday evenings, but still, you never know what kind of shit might go down. Ice, you'll be with Tango." The man nodded at the tall SEAL standing next to him. "Everyone comes home, gentlemen. We will take this shit seriously, but I want that asshole out of business, and I want to get back to my woman."

Chuckles were heard around the room, and they all smiled, nodding in his direction. For most, it had been nearly eight years since they wore a uniform, some more recently, but they still geared up like they were going to war. That's why they had an advantage over the Warriors. They were preparing like

warriors, not amateurs.

Comment [PC]: Here Zulu is identified as Delta.

Ditching the bikes for the evening, they piled into the waiting trucks and SUVs, Ace, Gunner, and

Blade traveling alone. The sixty miles to Warriors' territory felt longer tonight, but they all knew that

this problem with the Warriors needed to end tonight. It was cold and windy, the mountains definitely

giving them cloud cover, fine flakes of snow falling, but fortunately, not enough to stick. Still, it made it

cold and miserable if they had to go in by ground.

"Ghost, you hear me?" came the voice of Zulu.

"I hear you, brother." All heads turned sharply, everyone with communication devices linked to

the men currently on-site.

"Scar just arrived with the five boys we need, plus two more he just put in the warehouse. My

guess is he's hiding them inside just to be sure."

"Can you get to them?" asked Ghost.

"Don't insult me, asshole," said Zulu. "Yea, I can get to them. There's a roof entrance, which is

where I am now anyway. If I had to guess, one is probably going to come up here on his own. I'll tag

him and bag him, and then get to the other one. Hold tight."

Ghost waited patiently to hear from Zulu. The man was a former SEAL, so no doubt could

handle this little issue all by himself, but still, he hated that he wasn't there to support him. As a

member of the SEALs, Zulu received his name because he was always the last man in the line, just like

Zulu was the last letter in the call sign alphabet.

Trusted more than anyone to carry the rear of their team, he often kept dozens of insurgents at

bay while his team was able to complete their mission. He'd proven himself time and time again. When

Ghost was given the merged team of spec ops members, he asked for Zulu specifically. Now, more than ten years later, he was still one of his most trusted friends... brothers.

"It's done," came the voice. "Dudes were so fucking high they never even heard me coming."

"Thank you, brother," said Ghost.

"Five minutes out," said the voice of Gunner.

"Alright, everyone, lights off. We park down the road and walk in using the trees as cover. Ivan will be waiting for our call once we have them. Don't fuck this up!"

Gunner, Blade, and Ace made their way up the winding road, finally spotting the warehouse off in the distance. The only indication was the spotlight shining down on the front door. Blade made the turn easily and pulled up next to the bikes of Scar and the other members of the Warriors. He stepped from the vehicle, opening the door for Ace and Gunner, who straightened their suits.

"I assume you're Scar," said Gunner in his clipped accent.

"That's right," he smiled his tobacco-stained smile. "You must be Manfred."

"Correct. This is Mr. Grinkoff." Gunner pointed to Ace, who looked at Scar as if he were beneath him, taking in his dirty clothes and mottled face. The drug addiction was apparent, and even if they didn't hand him over to Anton tonight, he would be dead within six months.

"It's a pleasure," said Scar, sticking out his hand. Ace looked at the hand and then carefully slid his into the other man's.

"I'd like to see the merchandise," said Ace.

"Of course," Scar started to move to the warehouse. Hammer and the others following behind Gunner and Blade. "Right this way. I think you'll find we have everything you need here, sir. Thirty-seven cases of AK-47s, two cases of rocket launchers with ammo, four cases of grenades, one case of smoke bombs, eleven cases of nine-millimeters with ammo..." Ace held up a hand and nodded.

"Let me see," he said. Scar nodded, biting down hard on his lip. He opened the first case, and inside was exactly what he'd told them, AK-47s. They were military-issue, which meant that Scar somehow stole these from American bases or troops. If that was the case, Ace was having a hard time reconciling handing them over to Anton.

"What's the matter?" asked Scar in a disgusted tone. "You losin' yer nerve or something?"

"I don't lose my nerve, boy," said Ace.

"Oh fuck, everyone, get ready. Ace is losing his shit." Gunner, Blade, and Ace all heard Ghost's voice and knew that he was right. Ace needed to settle down, or the shit would blow too soon.

"I'm not your boy," said Scar, spittle flying from his face. "I've got the merchandise you want, and believe me, you're not the only one who wants it."

"Where are the drugs?" asked Ace.

"In another warehouse," said Hammer. Ace didn't even acknowledge his presence.

"Where?" he asked again.

"Just down the road. It's not that far..."

"Scar," warned Hammer. Interesting, thought Ace. Maybe Hammer was really running shit, and Scar was just the frontman.

"Is no matter. We take all," said Ace. "What about girls? You have girls?"

"Dude, do not fuck this up!" growled Ghost.

"We can get them for you. Got a game going with some friends in Pennsylvania. They get the girls for us, get 'em all primed and shit. We relax them with drugs, stretch those tight holes for your buyers, and you got a good shipment. I could get you ten or twenty by the end of the month."

"Maybe," said Ace.

"Why don't you show us the money?" said Hammer. Again, Ace didn't even acknowledge the man. Scar smiled, appreciating that someone recognized him as the talent in the organization.

"My associate gets ahead of himself sometimes, but we do want to see cash before delivery," said Scar.

Your friends are arriving now... we're blocking the back doors... masks down... we're coming in behind them.

Ace simply stood rock solid, still waiting for the door to open. As the handle turned, Hammer lifted his weapon, pointing it at the door while Ivan and Krevnyv walked in.

"What is this? What the fuck are you doing here?" yelled Scar.

"You owe me," said the older man. "You owe me, and this will be my payment." He waved his hand over the warehouse. Scar looked at Hammer and Digger, and then back at Anton and Ace.

"What the fuck is going on here?" asked Scar. The five men standing behind him felt a tap on the shoulder, all turning quickly only to have the butt of a rifle slammed in their faces. Like dominoes, they dropped together in a pile. Zulu and Gunner raced to secure their hands and feet while Anton watched in admiration.

"Well done, my friends," he said, smiling at Ace and Gunner.

"Friends?" said Scar frantically. "What the hell is happening here? Who are you?" He sounded like a pre-pubescent boy, his voice high and squeaky.

"Simple," said Ghost, standing before the man, his body encased in black armor, his face painted black, the black knit stocking cap covering his head. "This old SEAL just fucked you over. You're done, Scar. So are the Warriors."

"No! No, I have other men... other..." he looked around frantically.

"You mean these two?" asked Zulu, pulling the two to their feet. "You were told to bring five, and you brought seven. Not okay." Zulu secured Scar's hands and feet and then waited with the other men.

"We're done," said Ghost. "Do what you have to do." Anton nodded at Ghost, and then lifted his index finger in the direction of one of his men. One by one, he placed a bullet neatly in their foreheads, making his way down the line.

"Seven for the price of five," said Anton. "I love a good deal. We'll take the shipments now and then blow the warehouses as promised. Our deal is done." Ghost looked at the man and nodded.

"Our deal is done as long as you don't ever fucking come through my territory again." Anton laughed, a genuine belly laugh, as he tilted his head back.

"You are brave fucking American. You must be Ghost. I will not be in your territory again. I make promise for this. Have a wonderful evening, gentlemen. If you ever decide to make a little more money, come and see me. I could make you rich men."

"I'm already rich," said Ghost as he walked away. Ace, Gunner, and Blade got into the SUV and followed the walking men down the hill to their own vehicles. They waited as trucks passed, waiting for the warehouses to be emptied.

They didn't trust Anton as far as they could throw him, and they wanted to be sure the warehouses went up exactly as promised. Three hours later, the trucks passed once more, and a fireball could be seen for miles as the warehouse went up in flames. Two miles away another was seen, and three miles to the east of that still another.

"Let's go home."

CHAPTER FORTY

It was after five a.m. by the time they rolled back into the barn. The men all made their way to their own rooms, while Ghost, Tango, Doc, Zulu, Blade, Ace, Whiskey, and Gunner held back for a moment.

"Do you think we're done with him?" asked Tango.

"I sure as fuck hope so," said Ghost. "I think the bastard was actually impressed with us and what we did. I really don't give a shit either way. I don't want to cross paths with him again. The trackers should lead Homeland and the other members of the alphabet soup to him and whatever other stash he's got."

Axe and Ice entered the club, their bags on their backs. Ghost smiled at them both, their faces filled with relief.

"I take it you boys need a room," said Ghost, smiling.

"Yes, sir," said Ice. "Word got back to the club pretty quick, from an anonymous voice, of course, on what happened. You would have thought they were cockroaches the way they scattered. We were the last two to leave, decided to set the club on fire and let it burn to the ground. Didn't expect this," he said, tossing the bag at Ghost's feet. Axe followed, tossing his bag as well.

Kneeling, Ghost opened the bag and stared up at the men.

"Where the fuck did you get this?" he asked.

"It was in Scar's room. We checked to make sure there wasn't anything in the rooms, women mostly that might need help getting out, and found those two bags. Figured it might do some good for your club, help to track down more kids." Ghost eyed the two men carefully. Turning, he looked at the other men. Zulu stepped forward, gripping Ice by the neck.

"You tellin' the truth, boy?" he asked.

"Yes, sir, no reason to lie to you. We want to be a part of the club. We understand we have to be probies, and we're okay with that." Zulu nodded, turning to the others.

"Not how it works here," said Doc. "We don't do probies in the traditional sense. It's more like what you were used to in the military. You're new to this 'unit,' and we'll treat you as such. No stupid frat boy shit. You've both proven yourselves to us with this bullshit. Gunner will you show you to your rooms."

"Rules, sir?" asked Axe. Gunner raised an eyebrow in appreciation for the man asking in advance. Most guys would have just gone with what they knew and screwed up.

"Simple, we don't do drugs. You know that. This is a working bar and restaurant. No fucking women in the club. There are two steel doors to get to the private residences. Through the first, there are guest rooms. If you want to entertain a lady, use one of those. No one, and I mean no one, goes through the second door unless they live here." Both men nodded.

"Everyone works here. You either take your time at the garage, or you work the bar. We all work missions; you know that already. You'll be paid a salary commensurate with your job." Both men smiled, full tooth smiles.

"What are you smiling about?" asked Ghost.

"Umm, sorry, sir. The word commensurate, Scar wouldn't have known the meaning of the word. It's kind of nice to communicate in more than two syllables." Zulu laughed, and the others followed.

"You'll find that we're all educated and aren't afraid to show it," said Ghost. "I'm not saying we don't act like fucking savage animals sometimes, but well, you get it."

"Yes, sir, we sure do."

"That's the other thing. No sirs here. I'm not your commander. I'm your prez, just call me Ghost. That's it. Cool?" he said, sticking out a hand.

"Damn cool," said Axe, gripping the older man's hand. Ice did the same and then raised a brow.

"I assume that she is off-limits," said Ice, grinning at Ghost. They all turned to see a sleepy-eyed Grace coming towards them. She was wearing a pair of plaid flannel pajama bottoms and a sweatshirt that obviously belonged to Ghost.

"Under penalty of death, do not touch my woman," said Ghost. Grace wrapped her arms around Ghost's waist, kissing his jaw.

"Everyone okay? Everyone is safe? No one hurt?" she asked.

"We're all good, Gracie girl, and the mess with the Warriors is done," said Doc. "Grace, this is Ice and Axe. They'll be joining us."

"Hello," she said, smiling as she extended a hand, "welcome to the Steel Patriots."

"Thank you, ma'am," said Ice. Grace cringed and shook her head.

"Grace or Gracie girl, but never ma'am." Both men laughed, nodding at the petite woman. "Come to bed, Ghost. I have some things to talk to you about." Grace smiled at Ghost, winking at the men as she pulled him back towards the private quarters.

"No one better fucking disturb me. No one," said Ghost, following his wife.

"I think I'm going to like it here," said Axe.

"I know I will," said Ice, grinning.

CHAPTER FORTY-ONE

Grace pushed the tables together to create one long banquet table that would seat forty people. George placed two turkeys and a ham at one end and the same at the other end. There were huge warming trays filled with potatoes, gravy, yams, green beans, rolls, and cranberry sauce. All made from scratch by Grace and George.

The front door opened, and Bree walked in carrying a huge stack of sweets. Doc was the first to run toward her, taking the packages from her hands.

"Thank you," she said in a breathless voice. "I guess just put them wherever Grace wants dessert." He nodded as she followed him to the dessert table. Bree had really outdone herself, bringing an apple pie, cherry pie, and pumpkin pie, a tray of turtle brownies, and a long sheet cake with the most delicious cream cheese frosting ever.

Doc took her coat and swallowed as he took in the vision before him. Bree wore a lavender sweater that gently hugged her breasts, curving around her voluptuous body. The dark wool skirt fell nearly to her ankles, but it didn't deter from the vision of her mouth-watering hips. He was aching to touch her.

"You… you look beautiful," he said quietly.

"Thank you," she blushed. "You look handsome yourself. I've only ever seen you in t-shirts or leather." She smiled at him, and he nodded.

"Yea, my wardrobe is rather lacking. I actually bought this dress shirt and two others, along with some dress pants for the conference. I didn't want you to be embarrassed to be with me." Bree looked up at him, and her heart nearly stopped.

"Embarrassed? To be with you? Jack, can I call you Jack?" she asked. He nodded again. "I will be the envy of every woman at the conference... every woman in Toronto for that matter. You're the most handsome man I've ever met in my life, and I mean that with all sincerity. You could wear anything, and you would never embarrass me. I'm more worried that I won't be what you want. I mean, what you need. Not what you need..."

He held up a finger to her lips and silenced her.

"You are the most beautiful woman in the world," he said quietly, "and the only woman I give a shit about what she thinks about my wardrobe." Bree nodded her head, her cheeks now on fire. Doc leaned closer, closer... almost there...

"Dinner's ready!" yelled George.

"I'm gonna fucking kill him," growled Doc. Bree laughed but laced her fingers with his as they sat at the long table.

Grace and Ghost sat at the head of the table, smiling. Other than Bree, they'd told no one about her pregnancy and planned to announce it here today. They'd even chosen a name already, and Thanksgiving was the time to announce it.

"Happy Thanksgiving, everyone," said Grace, smiling as she tapped the water glass. "I'm so glad everyone decided to join us today. Hopefully, the house will be ready for a true Christmas celebration, but until then, this will do."

"We want to thank George for doing most of the cooking," said Ghost. Loud applause thundered in the room, and pats on the back were given to George, seated in the middle of the long table. "It's definitely a time of thanks. We welcome new friends, Axe, Ice, and Bree. We welcome you to our family." Doc squeezed Bree's fingers, and she smiled up at him.

"We welcome new loves," he said, grinning at Grace. "And we welcome new members." The room looked at one another. Bree said nothing, just smiling at Grace.

"New members… you mean Axe and Ice?" asked Doc.

"No," said Ghost, "I mean, Jack Tyran Stanton. My son, who will be born in just a few short months."

"Holy fuck…" said Tango.

"Son-of-a-bitch, he's multiplying," said Zulu.

"You… you're pregnant…" said Eagle. "You… you're naming him…" Grace moved around the table, touching the shoulder of Doc, and then standing in front of Eagle.

"You caught me that day, held me in your arms as you called for help. You may not remember, but I remember you whispering something in my ear. Do you remember what you said?" Eagle blushed, nodding, tears filling his eyes.

"I said you were going to be okay because only good men lived here and that you were too pretty to die." Throats bobbed up and down with emotion.

"That's right. You saved me, carried me into the arms of the man I would fall in love with. And you, Doc… Jack… you truly saved my life. Nursed me back to health. Will you both agree to be godfathers to our son, Jack Tyran Stanton?"

"Jesus, Grace, kill me, why don't you," said Doc, standing and hugging her to him. "Of course, I will."

"You know I will," said Eagle. "I can't wait to teach him all sorts of things." The mischievous grin on Eagle's sweet face made Grace laugh. Congratulations filled the air, and they all smiled at the couple.

"To us," said Ghost, "to our crazy-ass family, but it's ours."

"To us!"

EXCERPT from DOC

"So, what should we do first?" asked Bree. "I know there are some great restaurants here, shopping. The CN Tower is always cool if you're not afraid of heights." Doc couldn't help but laugh at her nervousness. The taxi was weaving its way through traffic, snow covering the ground.

"Why don't we get settled at the hotel and then make a decision. And for your information, Army Rangers don't get bothered by heights. It's sort of a job requirement," he laughed.

She smiled back at him, their fingers still linked together, just as they had been on the flight up. They'd yet to do anything except have a simple kiss on the cheek here or there, and Bree was beginning to wonder if all that sexy lingerie she bought when shopping with Grace was going to go to waste. As they pulled into the covered archway of the hotel, the taxi driver retrieved their bags and set them on the curb.

"Thanks," said Doc, handing the man a fifty. "Keep the change." The driver nodded, a big smile in appreciation.

The lobby was a large ornate space with massive chandeliers, soft music filtering through the speakers, and a positively delicious fragrance filling the air.

"How can I help you?" asked the man behind the desk.

"We have two reservations," said Doc. "One for Jack Harris and one for Aubrey Collins." The man pecked away on the keyboard, looked at the screen, and then pecked away again. Bree smiled nervously at Jack and then looked around the lobby once more.

"I'm sorry," said the man, "it seems there's been an error. We have one room available, and that's all. We're completely sold out."

"That's not possible," said Bree. "I have the confirmations right here." She spouted off the numbers, and the man nodded at her.

"Yes, I see the reservations, and I'm so terribly sorry for this, but I only have one room."

"Damn," said Doc. "Well, I can try to get something at another hotel."

"I'm afraid most of the hotels are sold out, sir," said the desk agent. "We have four conferences happening right now in the city, and it's the holiday season. We're always busy here this time of year. You could probably find something further away from the city."

"No," said Bree, "no, that doesn't make sense. How many beds are in the one room you have available?"

"Uhhh, it's a king, ma'am." Bree looked at Jack and smiled.

"We'll take it."

Other Books by Mary Kennedy you might enjoy!

REAPER Security Series
Erin's' Hero
Lauren's Warrior
Lena's' Mountain
Sara's' Chance
Mary's Angel
Kari's Gargoyle
Rachelle's Savior
Adele's Heart
Tori's' Secret
Finding Lily
Montana Rules
Savannah Rain
Gray Skies
My First Choice
Three Wishes
Second Chances
One Day at a Time
When You Least Expect It
Missing Hearts
Trail of Love

My SEAL Boys (connections to the REAPER Series)
Ian
Noa
Carter
Lars
Trevor
Chris
O'Hara

Strange Gifts Series
Dark Visions
Dark Medicine
Dark Flame

ABOUT THE AUTHOR

Mary Kennedy is the mother of two adult children, has an amazing son-in-law, and is grandmother to two beautiful grandsons. She works full-time at a job she loves, and writing is her creative outlet. She lives in Texas and enjoys traveling, reading, and cooking. Her passion for assisting veterans and veteran causes comes from a strong military family background. Mary loves to hear from her readers and encourages them to join her mailing list, as she'll keep you up-to-date on new releases at https://insatiableink.squarespace.com. You can also join her Facebook page at Insatiable Ink.

Dear Readers,

I love hearing from you and encourage you to visit my website Insatiable Ink. Leave me know your thoughts and ideas on new books or expanding on characters. It's also a safe space to give your own feelings, like those of the characters. I love reading about how you relate to the stories because as we all know, there's a little of each of them within us.

I look forward to hearing from you and hope you enjoy other books in my collections.

Explore... and enjoy!

www.ingramcontent.com/pod-product-compliance
Lightning Source LLC
Chambersburg PA
CBHW071510170626
46811CB00007B/2791